BREATHING LESSONS

BREATHING LESSONS

A novel

Andy Sinclair

ESPLANADE
Books

THE FICTION SERIES AT VÉHICULE PRESS

Published with the generous assistance of the Canada Council for the Arts
and the Canada Book Fund of the Department of Canadian Heritage.

Esplanade Books editor: Dimitri Nasrallah
Cover design: David Drummond
Photo of author: Carla Duffy
Typeset in Minion and Gill MT by Simon Garamond
Printed by Marquis Printing Inc.

LIBRARY AND ARCHIVES CANADA CATALOGUING IN PUBLICATION

Sinclair, Andy, author
Breathing lessons : a novel / Andy Sinclair.

Issued in print and electronic formats.
ISBN 978-1-55065-397-7 (pbk.). – ISBN 978-1-55065-406-6 (epub)

I. Title.

PS8637.I52B74 2014   C813'.6   C2014-908331-9
C2014-908332-7

Published by Véhicule Press, Montréal, Québec, Canada
www.vehiculepress.com

Distribution in Canada by LitDistCo
www.litdistco.ca

Distributed in the U.S. by Independent Publishers Group
www.ipgbook.com

Printed in Canada.

To Mom and Dad

Contents

HOW TO PLAY THE VICTIM

IN THE SUMMERS WHEN I was a teenager we lifeguarded at the beach, which was a pocket of land cut out of the forest. The sand was trucked in. The lake water wasn't polluted but it was smelly and brown from all the mulch. Nowadays people would call it organic. It was the kind of water that people from cities think is gross but if you poured it into a cedar-lined bathtub and lit a few pine-scented candles and advertised a Northern Waters Spa Experience, you could make a lot of money from those same people.

In the mornings the shadflies crunched underfoot as we swept them off the dock. Thursdays we came early for in-service training. We practised searching for lost kids, hauling unconscious people out of the water, splinting fractures. We did artificial respiration on each other, and there were no masks or resuscitation bags. If you played the victim, you had to let all your air out, and Becky, our boss, had to see your lungs expand when your rescuer breathed air back into you.

That was the summer a lifeguard in another town died when she got caught in a pool drain.

At our beach, the rafts and buoy lines were attached by thick rusting chains to heavy concrete anchors. What would happen, Becky asked, if you got caught down there? If your foot slipped underneath and you couldn't get back up? So we lined up, all twenty of us, and one by one dove down to the trapped victim. Nobody ever wanted to hang out at the bottom but me. It was quiet down there. I would exhale everything and sink ten or twelve feet into the reedy mud. Sometimes I'd see turtles swimming by and they'd pay me no mind. Then someone would come down—hunky Jeff from Montreal who worked with us because his stepmom had a cottage on the lake, my cousin Christine, my best friend Charlie. From the murk I'd see them break the surface and they'd spear through the sun rays to seal their lips around mine and fill me up. It was easy as long as you stayed relaxed and took it in. As long as you didn't choke you could go on forever.

I stayed under for fifteen minutes once before Becky gave the signal for me to come up.

That's teamwork, she said. That kind of effort can save a life.

When I tell people about this, they are sometimes shocked. Especially if they have kids. You could get a cold, they say. You could get herpes. Some of these people are guys who think nothing of walking into a dingy bathhouse at two in the morning, drunk out of their minds, for hours of messy sex. But it's okay because they're using *condoms*.

After the beach was closed, when it was dark, we'd all go back to hang out. We'd get drunk on Schooner's and take off our clothes and have all sorts of diving and running and handwalking competitions in the moonlight, our cold wet sunburnt bodies screaming to get laid. Jeff would bring girls behind the lifeguard shack and emerge later, sheepishly, glowing. He'd bring Christine back there sometimes and when it was over she'd look so grown-up and satisfied. That was my rookie summer. I was a few years younger than them and I knew I was jealous of her. But there were no words.

After a while we'd let the night air dry our skin and we'd put on our shorts and t-shirts. Then we'd open up the shack and sit in a circle and light a joint. The first time I didn't know how to inhale. What can I say? My Dad was the school principal. Charlie, who was experienced, raised his eyebrows invitingly and passed the spliff. I toked but felt nothing.

You're doing it wrong, said Christine. Quit taking little fish-puffs.

She was sitting next to Jeff. His big tanned hand rested on her thigh.

Here, Jeff said to me. I'll show you. Think of when we're under-water.

He inhaled deeply and held it in. Then he came over and sat in front of me and put his mouth over mine and exhaled. I could have come just from smelling him. Dark and sweet and musky. Salt and cream.

It hit me kind of instantly. I wasn't high and then I was high. A deep quiet hum and Jeff's warm breath tickling my ear. Faint stabs from his stubble.

Just take it in.

This was in front of everybody.

You might think this is going to be some story about a raunchy older dude breaking in a newbie, but it's not. I worked up the nerve later in the summer to ask him if he ever beat off.

No, man. I don't do that.

***

Now it's twenty years later and even with Facebook I am unfamiliar with the whereabouts of those people, even Charlie. I live in Toronto now and I'm a bit of the city softie I used to take pride in not being. I rejected a lot of notions but after a while some of them didn't seem so bad.

I go to yoga and practice my ujjayi breathing. The instructor Ron says to imagine we are fogging up a mirror. My head is a conch shell with the ocean breeze flowing through it. Ron says this type of breathing will rid us of toxins which from a physiological perspective doesn't make sense but I believe it anyway. He kneels over me while I am in child's pose and places his strong paws on my ribs.

Breathe into my hands, Ron says, and I feel like a selfish guppie but I do it and sometimes I get a bit choked up but other times I get this warm pleasant feeling in my chest, like there's a warm golden ball resting comfortably there. I'm sensitive, I guess, like everybody else. Once during a snowstorm nobody showed up but me so we did partnered asanas. I lay across Ron's back and we synchronized our breathing. I tried to concentrate but wondered if things might go pleasantly wrong. We slid out of the pose and our backs were still touching and I thought if I turn around now something will happen, but I didn't turn around.

Later that night I am at the Beaver with my homies. We go there to drink and laugh and talk dirty but I end up on the tiny dance floor in a mess of sweaty men. The DJ's spinning crazed shit, mashing Robyn with Arcade Fire and Neil Young with Chemical Brothers but it's working and I'm kinda drunk in a vague nebula, rag-doll arms. At the front of the bar, fat snowflakes thud against the steamy windows. In a moment of clarity I look around and everyone is lost in the music because it is so fine. This never happens. And then something else that never happens happens and this biggish young Daddy-type is vibrating right next to me nice and gentle. This isn't a full-on club—the shirts stay on but his is light cotton and his pecs cling to the fabric. Here is a real man and I'm tired of needing nothing. His forearm keeps bumping into mine and resting on it and when the music really thumps I draw my head into his chest and we pump it out for a while, mouths near ears.

Do you wanna go smoke a joint? It seems to be the new pick-up line in my circles. We're turning into a bunch of stoners.

I forget who even said it. Then we are in the cab, my left leg pressing into his right, the taxi clearing tracks through the snow-blanketed streets. We get out at the all-night store near my place because we don't have a lighter. I pick out a black one with a painting of a naked chick on it. Two girls with pancake makeup and tan woollen trench coats are buying hummus and pita bread and eyeing us like we are the ones with the problem.

Then we are in my apartment. He's brought his own spliff, in a tiny Ziploc.

We sit on the couch and he lights up and inhales. Then he grabs the back of my head and kisses me and fills me up. I take it all in, and let it out slowly. I take a puff myself. I sit in his lap, facing him, and we kiss again and I let my smoke seep inside him. I know how to give back now. His beard is salty from the dancing.

We sit in the curly haze. I watch the line of his muscled neck as it dives into his t-shirt. He looks down and starts rubbing my crotch. Then he smirks and looks right at me, squinting against the smoke. All sexiness and benevolence.

I should have warned you, he says, eyes shining. This shit makes you *horny.*

LIVE LIFE TO THE FULLEST

IT'S CHRISTMASTIME, and my younger brother Jeff and his son Luke and I are assembled at my parents' house. Luke is almost three and still doesn't talk much, so my brother has been egging him on with questions.

"Yum, Luke, I like pizza! Do you like pizza?"

"Yes."

"Did you like tobogganing with Uncle Henry?"

"No! Too fast."

"Next time we'll slow down."

I come into the kitchen where Luke and my parents are making animals out of coloured play dough. Luke reaches up to my father's forehead and presses on a green worm. It sticks and everybody laughs. My brother seizes upon the occasion.

"Luke, I love Grandpa. Do *you* love Grandpa?"

"Yes!"

I know I'm biased but this kid's a fucking angel. He's the only person I know who can just make me stop what I'm doing to feel the glow. He's usually charming, but today we are driving home from swim time at the Y and the chlorine has given him the sniffles and itchy skin. He is stuffed into his parka and strapped into his car seat like a miniature mental patient, and his nap is overdue. Then it starts to snow, so my brother turns on the squeaky windshield wipers.

"Stop those things!"

"Stop what things, Luke?" It's hard to tell if Jeff gets a kick out of this. "Stop what things?"

My nephew screeches in despair. "I don't know the *WORD!*"

I have run home for the holidays. I could have gone to Puerto Vallarta to hang out with a gay posse, but my inclination fizzled. They've worn me out with their heroic efforts to be noncommittal and ethical and fulfilled.

"I really like you," I said to the last one, Kevin. He's an immigration lawyer. Big lips and hands and smooth skin and a successful realtor boyfriend. We'd met through friends and buried the initial attraction and everybody knows what that does. Soon came the little friendly shoulder squeezes. Lingering hugs at the door. Sometimes it's just a matter of waiting until you are together alone, and stoned.

"I really like getting fucked up with you," he replied. We'd been experimenting with some coke that my neighbour had dropped off. ("Get this out of my sight," the neighbour had said, handing me a little baggie after knocking at my door. Six o'clock at night and he was in a bathrobe and looking wan and terrified. "My Christmas is over.")

I want it right in front of the city, I'd said, so we started at the balcony and then we fucked all over the apartment and finally I was face down on the bed and Kevin just pounding and I wondered if I'd be able to get out of it. I tested him to the right and left and he was too powerful. Holding me down, first in a T and then with his arms wrapped around me. I whimpered like an injured puppy while his hairy body slammed into me. The tat etched across his chest in grunge calligraphy: *Live Life to the Fullest*. Doesn't everybody dream of being taken care of like this? The next morning there were lubed fingerprints all over the windows and the bed was four feet from the wall. Greasy spots on the rug and unsalvageable sheets.

"So I guess this means we're not gonna fall in love and run away together, eh?" I said.

We were lounging in bed and I felt Kevin's body contract. "We have a nice connection," he said, and I thought of USB ports. He put down his smartphone. "I'm not sure what you're after. I don't really know what love means. It's the same brain activity as the blow, you know." He held up the empty baggie as evidence.

"Well," I said. "I guess if you don't know what it is, you won't know if you feel it."

"I guess. Anyway, we have a great time. No need to screw it up with words."

"You're right," I said, "why use words?" Then I entered new territory for me, a new tone. "Why validate? Why talk at all?"

He looked at me and I guess he didn't like what he saw. He put his clothes on very quickly, like a superhero in reverse.

"Let me know when you grow up so we can start fucking again. I've gotta get home."

I have a good, easy insurance job and I go to lots of parties, good wild house parties that you can't pay to get into. I like to have a fun time but my only addiction is to hot yoga. Somehow, though,

I have turned romantically destitute. I think of this while my nephew and I build a space shuttle with Lego, lying on my parents' living room floor. There are specialty pieces for everything— exhaust pipes, the Canadarm, tiny space helmets. Each with a sole purpose. I'd say it's too bad that it's so regimented but it's satisfying when the pieces lock in place. Besides, I don't want to be a Luddite. I got an iPhone. I got myself hooked up on Grindr—paid for a membership. Hot guys at ten, twenty, fifty metres. A cornucopia of muscular chests and handsome faces and big cocks. What are you supposed to do with all that? A lot of the chat goes nowhere but sometimes the guy is right there in real life—you can see him checking his phone. The last time I hooked up that way the dude just wanted to suck cock. He offered me a Blue Light and a King-size Marlboro and I sipped my beer and watched the World Series while he worked me over. He lived in a small, rundown studio and had two cats and a string of coloured lights along one wall and it was all friendly and mild and novel.

I run a bath for Luke. He gets in with the space shuttle and I stick my face right in the water and blow violent bubbles. Space-quake. The tub vibrates and my nephew screeches in his singsong voice.

"Again!"

"Again!"

"Again!"

Thrills and screams, over and over. I can rock somebody's world after all. This goes on for so long that we have to keep refilling the tub to warm it. His exhausted single father is net-surfing in bed, in a room that could only exist in some adult's parents' house: popcorn brocade quilt, wood-carved *paysan* lamp, delicately-flowered wallpaper and an oil landscape that my uncle painted in 1968. I hope Jeff's looking around on Lavalife or something but I doubt it. He's become too wary. My mother is already asleep after a frenzied day of playing with her grandson, and my father is snoozing in front of the news. My brother and I are in our thirties.

I slept like death after the first time with Kevin. His boyfriend was out of town so he stayed over. When I woke up we were facing each other and our limbs were all pleasantly entangled. I could smell his musky sweat and I looked down along his humpy body at the big soft cock nestled against my leg and got a sweet vertigo. I thought of the slow deep kissing and the fucking, every orifice in play. Plugs and sockets. *We have a nice connection.*

I extract Luke from the tub and dry him off. We exclaim over his wrinkled fingers, but now he's fading. He has gone from wildly hyper to barely conscious in about thirty seconds. I manage to wrangle him into his sleeper, then I pick him up and bring him to his father.

At the door, Luke wraps his arms tightly around my neck and nestles his face into my chest.

My brother sees this and can't resist a teaching moment. "Luke, I love Grandma and Grandpa and you and Uncle Henry. Do you *love* Uncle Henry?"

One last dreary brain squeeze before Luke can collapse into sleep. He lifts his soft little head to think about it. He looks up at my face and I smile down but my grip on him has tightened.

While he considers, I wait.

EVERYTHING FLOATS AT DIFFERENT LEVELS

CRAIGSLIST IS THE ONLY PLACE I can find guys who are into this kind of sex. I don't meet anybody at the bars anymore, or through friends. I appreciate a nice body at the gym and I get turned on in the showers watching soapy water slide down muscle. I'll even turn it to cold, especially if somebody is showing off a big dick.

But I never get leg-shaking lust, not even when some hottie is staring me down. The only type of guy I want is rough.

This finally came out in Group. Brendan the nerd likes to score points with Josh, the mediator, so he has to stick his hand up a lot.

"There are various social, economic and political reasons for your choices," he says. No shit. He's taking poli sci at York. "Maybe it's because you are white, or maybe it has to do with your parents' level of education. Who knows? You don't have to understand the causes, but you have to identify *a pattern* in order to stop the behaviour."

Josh blinks. "It's important to speak in I terms, Brendan. Henry, do you agree?"

I'm tired of Brendan. His back is too straight, and the irony of the thick-framed glasses seems lost on him. "There are various social, economic and political reasons for everything," I say. "But I am tired of you being such a geek."

Josh says we should move on now.

I signed up for Same-sex Relationship Issues at the community centre because I thought there might be somebody fuckable in the group, but no. We are all just too sensitive. There was one guy, Alan, who seemed like he had potential, but I knew he wasn't going to do it for me when I saw he was wearing Aussie Bum underwear. He let me suck him off but then afterwards he wanted to cuddle.

Amanda at work likes to check in on me. She wanted me to call the police last time because my forearms were all bruised. But it was just from the guy gripping. I have thin skin.

"Why do you go after guys like that?" she said, hovering over my desk while I tried to pull my sleeves down. I'd forgotten to send a thank-you gift to a client but she'd done it on my behalf. The tips of her soft limp hair touch the edge of the file I'm working on. She has nice breath. She's tall and pilates-thin and has no love life. She looks like Feist.

"You're so smart, Henry. So together." She is not to be trusted. "Why do you let them treat you that way? There must be a *reason*."

I should sic Brendan on her. She arranges lunch with me for tomorrow, walking away silently in her argyle skirt and thick wool tights, a shy smile as she looks back at me one last time before retreating to her cubicle. I like her, she is my confidante at this stuffy place that overcharges and overpays and uses too-thick carpeting, but she could use a good fuck.

After I leave the office, I go home and start trolling through the ads. I click on *Black Muddafucka (38)—downtown*. There is no pic. *Big fascist pig want to rape white faggot—boy pussy*, it says. *Five-ten, one seventy, eight inches*. Whatever. None of those numbers ever mean anything. I like his attitude, though.

I write back, *sure would like to meet you. Twink, 29, 5'8", 140, blond, blue, 7c. Hosting near Little Italy. U travel?*

He waits before responding. I try not to think about it. I try not to let my imagination get out of control. Most guys are putting on a facade. Even if they show up they probably aren't going to be what you'd expected. But due to various social, political and economic reasons, I hope.

Inbox (1). He wants my address. I live in one of those rats' nests condo buildings with concierge so I don't care about getting mugged. He leaves me waiting for a long time, over an hour, and I start to be disappointed and relieved, but then he buzzes.

He smiles at the door but when I help him off with his coat and I'm about to offer him a drink he shoves me on the bed and starts pulling down my pants.

"Nice butt," he growls, and slaps it, then again like he's tenderizing a piece of meat. He slides his jeans off and the belt buckle makes a heavy clank on the floor. Then he gets on top of me and turns me onto my back. He crawls over me and shoves his dick in my mouth. It's goes from fairly soft to hard quickly, like a balloon filling up with air. He doesn't say anything. I gag a little but that's it. We are both oddly quiet and efficient—no moaning noises. We follow the script—I keep working his cock. He wasn't lying about the eight inches. I'm on my knees, my back, my side, getting him ready and I'm glad I drank a lot of water today and that I didn't have a pre-fuck toke. If I'd been stoned my mouth would be dry and this would not have worked so well.

He flips me over, bites my cheeks, blows in my hole, then rubs

23

his chin stubble right over my sphincter. I finally say something, O God. He sticks his tongue in and out, laps along my crack like a hairy lizard. Then he sticks a finger in and I gasp.

"You'd better be able to take it."

He puts the condom on, lubes up. I remember what they said at Youthline when I called. *Push like you're taking a shit and it won't hurt.* So counter-intuitive but it's always worked. He doesn't really pay attention to my reactions. He just shoves it in and starts pumping. He keeps me on my stomach the whole time, grunting and with my neck in the crook of his arm, his fist against my temple. My chin rests on his big slick bicep. I lick it and taste salt and he pulls my hair and tells me not to do that. But I can tell he's not really angry, he's playing a game, too. The actual fucking doesn't last long, maybe three minutes.

But it's an excellent three minutes.

I debate asking him if he wants a beer after but worry that he'll say yes. I don't want to find out he's an accountant in the office down the street, or a chiropractor. After he leaves, I tidy up and have a shower. I soap off the lube and scrub the crusty cum from my stomach. Then I get out and throw the bedding in the wash. I enjoy the whole clean-up. I usually stop in the middle of it and jerk off, remembering and revising. I wish his fist had been a cold heavy gun.

A long time ago, I remember a knife. It was the summer I was fifteen, and staying in a university residence downtown for a science camp. On Charles Street. We didn't lock our doors. I'd spend my days working on Bucky Ball models and measuring out frog intestines. I don't know how the guy got in the main entrance, but he ended up in my room. He was big and black and had a switchblade. It's not like in the TV re-enactments, all grainy and blurred. It's not about what it looks and sounds like, anyway. It's about how it makes you feel.

24

"Where is your money?" he said, and I handed it all over. I could have screamed. There were other people on that floor. I was hyper-alert and still. I was waiting for it to end, I think, or to see where it would go. I could feel my heartbeat in my head. I could hear it, too. It wasn't torturous. I was very, very awake.

He put the money in his pocket very calmly. Then he came over to where I was sitting on the bed. He took off my shirt and used it to tie my hands behind me. I was obedient, and mesmerized that someone could be so brazen. Then he pulled my pants down.

"I'm going to rape you," he said.

I remember finally screaming soon after that. Then there was a scuffle, shouting, gaps. A policeman was untying my hands and I was sitting on the bed, my pants still down around my ankles. One of them took me to a pay phone to call my parents but only my little brother's babysitter was home. I'd been fine until then but when I went to talk nothing came out. Each time I opened my mouth my throat constricted. The officer had to come on the line and arrange everything. My parents drove down the next day and brought me home. My mother getting out of the car, the first time I saw her as a person. She wasn't wearing a scarf over her head but I remember her that way. Something beyond anger or sorrow or protection in her stoop, something infinitely dark that had to do with me.

Back home, I was a minor celebrity for a while. I got to fly back to Toronto with my parents for the trial. We stayed in the Hilton and I had my own room. In court I had to point to his cage. I don't know if he looked at me at all. He'd been high, they said, and they'd picked him up at the bus station. When they asked me what happened I got the information out, my voice shaking, sniffling, everything blurred and my eyes cool. After, my father told me I had been very brave, which made no sense at the time. I can picture him in his best suit, trying to catch my eye and speak in the gentle, reassuring, capable voice of a good country gentleman. I don't think I could've stood it.

I came out a few years after that.

My best friend asked if this had anything to do with that time I went to science camp, like it could be reasoned away so tidily, as if my realization had nothing to do with my tussles with him on the lawn.

"No," I said. "I'm *gay*." It was only much later, after we'd lost touch, somewhat deliberately, that the question enraged me, and I only remembered that because my older brother Doug, the cop with the Master's in forensic psychology, asked almost the same thing when he came to get me after the last break-up. A seven-hour drive to the small port town. Coke-addict fisherman boyfriend. Scaring me out of my wits. The boyfriend had taken the chainsaw to the front porch and I honestly thought he was going to use it on my neck next.

"You keep getting into these fucked-up relationships," my brother said. "Does this have anything to do with that guy in Toronto?"

I shrugged and looked out the window. I had been rescued again.

"I have never felt so helpless as when that stuff happened," he said, and I hadn't had any clue about that. I wondered why I have always taken them for granted, like I could leave all my problems hanging in the air for them to shoo away. I remember when we went camping when I was little and our dog Gracie came in the canoe with Doug and my mother and me. Gracie hated that canoe but it was a calm day and my mother wanted her to get used to it. My mother swam beside the canoe, long expert strokes, but when she tried to climb in Gracie went crazy, barking and jumping, and we tipped. All my mother's clothes, our sun hats and towels, all fell overboard and while my mother and I clung to the side of the canoe and tried to calm Gracie, my brother swam down beneath the surface and collected everything.

"What was it like down there?" I'd wanted to know but had been too afraid to go deep.

"It was neat," he said. "Everything was just sort of floating at different levels. I guess it depends on the density of the fabric. It was like ghosts were holding everything up, like in a haunted room." And as we kicked the canoe in towards shore (which wasn't very far away, there hadn't been any real danger), I envied him.

I haven't talked about Charles Street in Group, though I know it's key. I just don't want to shatter Brendan's world, maybe. Or feed his obsessions. He'd want to know if I was bullied in school, too. Around puberty, maybe? In the locker room? He'd wave his Psych 100 textbook in front of my face and tell me it was obvious.

Last Friday I took the back streets home from the Beaver because I was drunk. I hadn't been on Charles Street forever and I barely recognized it. The old residence had been torn down. They'd sold the land for a condo tower and the excavating had already started in earnest. The whole area was partitioned off. *Danger due to Construction.* Posters on the boarded fence—Madonna night at Fly, Radiohead at the Air Canada Centre, political docs at Cineforum. I stumbled off my bike in the streetlight to have a look through one of the little windows that they had cut out but there was nothing there, just a deep hole. Even through the soft boozy haze I felt uneasy. I could peer in, but I couldn't see the bottom.

WE'RE JUST LIKE EVERYBODY ELSE!

JEFF, MY COKEHEAD BROTHER, has cleaned up his act because of his three-year-old. He hasn't touched the stuff since he found out his ex-wife was pregnant. Or he's at least kept it on the downlow.

"After you have kids," my mother says on the phone, by way of explanation for this thirty-two-year-old who has caused her hair to whiten prematurely and used up a good deal of my parents' money in rehab and probably brought them a good fifteen years closer to death, "there comes a certain maturity."

Then, catching herself, "I didn't mean—"

Me: "Never mind."

My mother: "Oh, honey, your father and I just love you."

I guess I would have had kids if I'd been straight. But I'm not, and I'm also not an assimilationist. Also, after rent, the car, and various fucking-around sundries there's not much left over, certainly not enough to pay for diapers.

"But you do it together with someone," Jeff says. Like who? I've only had one real relationship that lasted beyond a couple of weeks, and that one was with a manic-depressive. It only hung on because the prospect of leaving seemed so exhausting. Anyway, everyone used to say you couldn't be gay and have a kid, because that was irresponsible and confusing and would fuck it up. It's okay if you want to be that way but you shouldn't be imposing that on someone else. Even my mother would have agreed with that, then. Now they've changed their minds, they think homos are so loving and gentle and *nurturing*. But I'd read some Thomas Kuhn in the interim, and I know they might take it all back. Besides, the gays had it right before, when they lived on the margins. Now it's different—we're just like everybody else! Except we're really, really into cock. We're not supposed to slut around on the internet or at the tubs, though. Or talk about it.

"You fall in love when you have a baby," says Jeff. "I knew I'd always wanted to be a father, but I never knew it would be this amazing." It's true, I've watched him pick up his kid after naptime, my brother's eyes all glassy and insane and loose around the edges. That's as sure a sign as any. He says that after Luke was born he would just sit and watch him all day. In awe, I guess. In adoration. Like even more than for those NHL stars and Olympians. Even I cried when Alex Bilodeau was on the podium. The networks really loved his brother, too. I hate to be a cynic, but that was a coup.

Jeff says he can't really describe parenthood. It's something you have to *experience*.

"Luke's brought me on a *journey*," he says. "Anything that happens to him, happens to *me*." And he looks at me with those converted, earnest little-brother eyes that the chicks dig so much, like nothing he says is to be interpreted as critical or offensive.

29

Because we're family.

I'm happy for my brother. But he tries to explain it to me like I've never felt intense love, which isn't true. Like the other day this twenty-year-old from Manhunt was squirming underneath me, moaning sweet nothings. He'd said his name was Ken.

Fuck man your dick just feels so right, he said, as I was sliding in and out. *Feels so good. I love that cock.*

And then, as he was coming, *I love you. Oh, I love you.*

Some people might say that that's not love but I can tell you our eyes were shiny and glassy and we looked insane. I know that because the glass doors on my broken old closet are mirrored, and they do not lie.

Everybody talks so admiringly about my brother now.

"He just always wanted to be a father," they say. "Even when he was little. You could tell." I find this odd, since I was the one interested in dolls. I wasn't allowed to play with them, though. The shaky new belief that toys needn't be gender-specific had not quite reached my parents.

I'm up in East Shore for the long weekend. What long weekend? *Family Day.* A perfectly arbitrary, jurisdictional and political occasion. No matter—I love my family. It's Saturday, and Jeff—who unbeknownst to me WAS trawling through the online personals— and his new girlfriend Manon have gone for an impromptu ski across the lake. My mother, who usually babysits, has a salon appointment. Normally she'd reschedule, but her hair has been disappointing her lately, and since my father has bridge, Luke is left in my care for the afternoon at my parents' place. I am at least an adequate uncle, possibly a good one. I am perhaps slightly haphazard when it comes to minor safety issues but I feel the risk so far has been worth the excitement.

Luke's picking his nose, and I figure he gets enough discipline from his parents, so to distract him I fart loudly and he stops picking and laughs and claps his hands.

"*Encore!*" he says. Manon is trying to teach him French, even though Luke can barely speak English. But he loves to play. Unfortunately, I only had one in me to rip so I crank up *Allergies* by Barenaked Ladies and start to chase him. The living room is connected to the den, which connects to the dining room and back to the living room. I follow him around this circle, faster and faster, his little legs spinning and his hair blowing in the wind. I want him to associate me with exhilaration, not drives to daycare or baking cookies. To surprise him, I reverse direction, but I do it too quickly and he slides on the hardwood floor into a head bump with me. He's fine, just a bit shocked, and he almost starts to laugh before deciding on a big howl. I pick him up and massage his soft little forehead. Magic rub.

I turn the music off and sit down as he clings to my chest. He sniffles. He's okay.

"I hurt," he says.

I don't say anything.

When I get home, Ken comes over. The sex is pretty fantastic again. Usually, I like to get up right after and get everything wiped off and show the guy out, but he puts his head on my chest as soon as he comes and I go with it. I'd left the hockey game on and we lie there in the dark and listen to the play-by-play in the next room, our cum drying into a crust on my stomach. His head feels so light. All his hair is ginger-coloured, and his long eyelashes tickle my nipples. I doze off a bit and wake up to Don Cherry not-apologizing for talking politics. Then I listen to Ken's breath a bit before I start shuffling around with my gotta-busy-day-tomorrow routine.

When he's leaving, he pauses at the door.

"We should do something this week," he says. He stands there, lean and confident and knowing, with his beret and smartly-knotted scarf. He grew up downtown.

"Uh, yeah," I say. "Like, here?"

"Yes," he laughs. "But I mean, before."

"Sure," I say. "Maybe."

But I've got time Thursday evening so we meet up at the skating rink at Ryerson. We glide around the big boulders and I teach him how to go backwards. He's not a bad skater, but he never played hockey. He didn't want to and nobody made him. He doesn't want to get in the way of all the guys shinnying but I tell him it's fine, there's room for all of us. He keeps looking up at the shifting coloured panels on the new art school.

"Would you rather be looking at pretty colours than learning how to skate?"

"Yeah," he says. "They're turning me on."

We don't stay much longer. After I've driven us back to my place Ken sits on the couch and rolls us a joint while I make hot chocolate and check the messages. One from my brother, *Luke said he had a great time with you on Saturday. When the fuck are you gonna do it again? He keeps asking.* The other from my father, *Mom and I heard that Luke's your biggest fan. Proud of you, bud!*

We share the joint and sip our drinks. I added brandy to mine but Ken didn't want any. While we're waiting for the pot to kick in I screw a special light bulb into the bedroom lamp. The room lights up porn-style, all shades of red.

We make out on the bed and I try to go slow but it's too good. I just want to get inside that ass. I tear his clothes off and eat him out and slip on a condom and ease in. I grab his hand away from his dick, which he'd been rubbing, because I don't want him to come too fast. The pot is enhancing everything and I just want to do this for a long time. I reach inside my nightstand drawer for poppers. We take some generous inhales, and then I just pound and pound and pound.

Oh, he says. I love you. His voice is all muffled in the pillows.

He's lying right down on his stomach and I've gotten him nice and loose. I pull all the way out and then shove right back in, and each time he says, yes, Daddy. I guess I'm old enough to be called that. I have a few white hairs on my chest. I can't say it bothers me.

I flip him over and we fuck face-to-face and we both get glassy-eyed again. I watch him in the red dimness, his eyes shining right at me, some feral animal in there, lost and found. Then his face scrunches up and he comes.

That's it, I whisper. *That's it, baby.* I've watched so much porn that sometimes I can't tell if I'm just repeating stuff or if it's coming from inside me, but I feel amazing.

I stay on top of him after I shoot and we fall asleep like that. We wake up in the dead of the night and flip positions in the dark, me putting the condom on him. He's never been the top before and I guide him in. It doesn't take him long to come, in one big long shudder. The sheets are soaked in lube and cum and sweat. I rip them off and throw down a flat sheet and we lie back down. I watch him while he sleeps, his smooth face all peaceful. He wakes up a bit and reaches around me and holds me tight. We're still like that in the morning.

He asks why I don't have a boyfriend.

"Dunno," I answer. "Why don't you?"

"Oh," he says, "I've had a few. But I dumped them because the sex wasn't exciting enough." And he gives me a shit-eating grin and a wink.

He's quiet for a minute. Then he tells me it's his birthday next week.

"I wanna mark the occasion by getting fucked by two guys at once," he says.

I smile. "Really?"

"Yeah," he says. "I want two dicks just filling me up. I want to try everything. You want in on that?" This child is wild.

"Sure," I say. I may as well come along for the ride with this guy. You only live once.

I guess it's been more than a few weeks now.

I know what my little brother would think if he knew all this. He'd ask me when am I gonna drop the sexually-obsessed gay thing? We all have to grow up sometime, he'd say. He'd tell me to get a dog, and that it's immature to be so caught up in frivolity, and that until you are responsible for the life of another, you will never truly be a man.

I'd say whatever, Jeff. You're the one who always wanted to be a daddy.

PEOPLE WHO SENSE SADNESS STAY AWAY

FROM THE BALCONY, I CAN SEE Joe cycle up Yonge Street, a joint hanging off his grin. He's been coming to visit us quite often lately. He rides his bike upright. The ones you fall for barely ever use their handlebars.

He goes way back with my boyfriend Perry. They were only teenagers when they started go-go dancing at the same club. That was almost fifteen years ago. Perry was a runaway, practically a street kid, and Joe wasn't much better off. They'd coke themselves up and go to work and snort more coke. After work, they'd do more coke and then go to an after-hours club and snort more, more, more. Come sunrise, a bunch of guys would all crash at one place and have group sex, penises penetrating holes haphazardly. Or at least that's my understanding of it. Perry told me they would get paid three hundred dollars a night and there would always be a negative cash flow. Now they just smoke a lot of dope and work odd jobs. Joe does painting and repairs; Perry caters and bartends and does a bit of drug-dealing. And, five years ago, they each acquired a stable, boring boyfriend: Perry got me and Joe got Alan.

Perry says that Joe had a beautiful body back then. Everybody wanted a piece of him. I know they were lovers, too, although I don't know if either of them would use that term. As I said, I think sex for them was an afterthought, something to do when there were no more drugs. Something not directly sought or planned for, and inevitable. This is altogether different from my own experience—at that age, I sought and planned, in my own incompetent way, to no avail. I know I wasn't ugly; I just didn't know how to look at a guy the right way. I'd only been with a few guys before I met Perry.

Joe's just finished painting the bedroom deep red. Perry wanted the colour changed because our sex life is boring, but I don't think that's going to fix anything. After Perry goes to work, I sit on the couch with Joe. We've snuck a Temazapam each from Perry's stash and we're tranced out, bowling on Joe's cell phone, passing it back and forth. I can't tell if his hand lingers on mine or not. Perry would be furious. Nothing happens.

In my languor, I feel like going for a swim, so Joe walks me to the Y, guiding his bike expertly over the crusts of snow and ice on the sidewalk, holding just the seat with one hand.

He asks me if I ever sleep with other guys. It's a risk to answer yes because he might just be fishing, for Perry's sake. But I know he's not.

"A few times, when I've been away at work," I say. Icy beer and a warm hard body. It really has happened only occasionally. I've heard Joe used to be a total slut—whenever he's late meeting us, Perry says he's probably met a random guy on the street. No one ever talks about this in front of Alan, who seems genuinely oblivious.

The times I've done it, it's always been the same. A smell of celebration, fake names. Something sleazy and good, but cold, too. I used to think I was defying convention but I was kidding myself. You're supposed to be doing those things, or at least some people think so.

"That's good," says Joe.

Joe hangs out with Perry and me the next few days but now Perry's gone to wait tables. It's dark and we decide to assess the looks of the bedroom. City lights on red paint. Tension, muscles listening. All afternoon I could feel my body waiting to be alone with him. Then, alone, we have to wait to make sure no one comes back for a forgotten subway ticket, or corkscrew.

"I've been thinking of you," I say.

"I've been thinking of *you*."

"What were you thinking?"

"That I I like you. What were *you* thinking?"

Too quickly to enjoy it much—was it what I'd thought it would be, or better, or not as good? Later I'll wonder if it will be worth the hurt, but for now there are only rising shadows, sweet breath. My hands on the back of his muscular neck. He runs his fingers through my hair.

"That was fun," he says after.

We are bowling again, on the cell phone. I have to try not to talk.

Joe and Alan invite Perry and me over for dinner. Joe and Perry have a smoke on the deck while Alan and I wash the dishes. Alan is smart and cute and not very sexy. He scrapes the chicken carefully off the grill while I dry the glasses. It's warm inside the kitchen, freezing outside. The steam from the dishwater condenses on the windows and Perry and Joe become a blur.

"I wonder what they're talking about," he says.

"Probably old times, as usual."

37

Alan keeps at his scraping.

"It's really hard to get these things clean," he says.

Alan works regular hours at the legal clinic but Joe works when he wants. I'm a flight attendant at a dying airline now, and winter's my low season—a couple of long turnaround days a week to the Caribbean are the most shifts I can get. On my days off, I tell Perry I'm going to the library to research careers, and head on over to Joe's. He greets me at the door and we kiss like I never, ever have. His body is impossible to remember. It seems waifish one day, but the next too big and humpy to reach around. He is either short or tall. If someone asked me if he was fat, I wouldn't know what to say. I'm into him, though. I know that.

"You sure do like going to that library," says Perry, when I get back to the apartment. "I missed you."

He is counting out pills like a kid sorts Smarties. He has all sorts of doctors and all sorts of pills—lorazepam and valium, Percocet and Prozac. Business is thriving. Maybe he'll be able to cover his share of the rent for once.

"What do you want for dinner?" he asks, and I ask him what we have.

"Nothing," he says. So I go buy groceries.

A weekday. As usual, Joe jumped out of the bed as soon as he creamed. There was a bit of snuggling the first few times but he's stopped that without explanation. We're in the living room. I'm sitting on the couch and Joe is at the window, smoking. He's decided to repaint this room, and we're discussing colours.

"Red," says Joe. The afternoon light reflects off his eyes so that I can't see the pupils. His eyes are so pale and shallow, beaming blue. It's the first time I have ever looked at someone my age and thought of him as weathered and ageing. He's more attractive because of it.

But he changes his mind. "No, red's too angry. For a while, I wore it all the time." I think about the red walls with Perry. Joe means in his heyday with all his gang, when they went to weekend-long raves. When they all wore Mohawks and bicycle chains and safety pin piercings.

"I thought red was passionate," I said.

"No. Purple is passionate. Before red, I always wore purple."

"Because you wanted to be passionate?"

"Because I *was* passionate." Fierce certainty. The words cut me up, dark blood. I was thinking about how I wear a lot of blue, and all the time that was gone. But to feel some vitality again, that would be something. Before the blue came, a long time ago, I remember smashing my hands against the steering wheel, scream-ing to myself while I made breakfast, midnight runs, terrible desire.

There is pressure inside of me now. More than ever before. Soon I'll be starting arguments with people for no discernible reason. I remember this. This is what it feels like to be alive. It's what I want and I won't be sorry.

When I met Perry he was so down and I tried to help him be happy. I was twenty-four and new to Toronto. I didn't feel a bone-aching lust but what did I know? I'd heard from straight friends that it develops. Perry flattered me. One Monday morning I left his apartment and I said I was going to have a busy week and that I'd see him Friday and he just looked stricken with grief. He seemed to adore me unashamedly, and that was something I'd never come close to experiencing. It's true he used me—I just took it in when he screamed out his frustrations. That time we came out of Woody's and he walked up to that flyer kid, and yelled at him to get a real job, to quit littering the street with his dumb-ass pieces of paper. The kid was scared and I told Perry to leave him alone but he wouldn't listen to me. That innocent kid. I know it was coming from somewhere else. It always was.

Sometimes Perry just lay in bed all day. I made excuses on the phone for bosses, creditors, friends out of favour. Juggling all his lies. All those times I came home and he was spaced out on ketamines, rearranging the furniture.

"I've finally got it figured out," he'd say, pupils the size of dimes.

"Tell me," I'd say. But he could never remember what he'd been talking about once he'd come down.

I tried to keep him out of trouble. But I was using him as an excuse to give up.

I remember being with Perry, in an old borrowed truck. I was taking him to his hearing, an hour away. He'd lost his temper again at a party, and had smacked a guy, hard. And spit in his face. It's hard to say who overreacted, but the police came and laid assault charges.

Perry was backing the truck out of the garage for me because, even though his licence had been revoked, he was still, by far, the more capable driver.

The truck stalled dead and would absolutely not start up again. It looked as though we not be on time.

"We cannot be late, Perry," I said. "This is *court*. Do you understand that?!"

I'd forgotten that he would be stressed out himself. He got out of the truck. His face was all crinkled. Then he backed himself up against the wall of the parking lot. A little man, curling in and bending over. Hopelessness personified, right in front of me. I was thinking that this was what defeat looked like, right here, more than I've ever seen and much more than I'll ever feel myself.

I will do anything for you right now, I was thinking. I will get down on the ground and beg for all of your misery and troubles to end. I will find whatever you need and pay for whatever it takes so that I can stop witnessing this anguish.

And I was thinking that I would have to leave him soon, because he just needed me way too badly.

Later, in the rental car that I somehow obtained despite my maxed-out credit card, Perry told me that he couldn't do anything right and I disagreed, but only out loud.

Joe's decided on green for his living room. Alan comes home from work while Joe and I are painting. A legitimate visit even though we had sex between coats. Alan is maybe as much of an actor as me because he seems pretty happy. Joe gives Alan a kiss on the cheek, then the lips. Then Alan turns to go put his briefcase down and Joe grabs him from behind, dry humps his ass, tells him he's in heat.

Alan invites me to dinner. Joe is gregarious, charming. He serves the potatoes and kisses Alan's neck as he stands behind him, and he leaves his lips on Alan's skin for a great deal longer than a second. I chew my food nonchalantly, pretending to admire the paint. When I leave, Alan is in the study and Joe walks me to the door, kisses me ambiguously. I am conscious of my eyes showing need so I look down. We are all adults, I am thinking. We can do what we want and we don't need to justify anything to anybody.

I've been fantasizing about Perry committing suicide. It would solve a lot of problems.

"You'd be better off," he's said. How does he know?

He's tried it before, or pretended to have tried it. Same difference. Straddling the balcony, twenty-eight stories above our luminous city, accusing.

I shouted no and Perry swung himself down and came to me and asked me to hold him. That was real living, too.

"I don't have a family," he'd said a long time ago, so I offered to be that for him. Before I came along, his friends were his family, but they all died.

"I slept on the floor," he says. "I watched pus come out of them while I massaged their feet." He means that I don't have to put up with as much in comparison, but Perry's not dying. This could go on forever.

Now he is yelling at me again, something to do with some housework that I've performed poorly. The reasoning behind his argument is obscure but what is certain is that I am spoiled and rotten and cunty. He is either at the end of his rope or has forgotten our last conversation, the one where I made the vague threat that I was unhappy. I let him finish his rant and then go to our bedroom with a glass of wine and swallow it down with a sleeping pill. I lie down for twenty minutes, watching the red, until I am good and spinning. I come out to the balcony where he is glaring into space, chain-smoking.

This is it, right now.

All the best ones, like Joe, share the same laugh. They all smile secretly to themselves, remembering. The smile of someone who has always done what he's wanted, delicious erotic encounters that you haven't had yourself because you don't have the same life force; that's the attraction. Joe has confidence. Complete assurance. As easy for him to stare someone down and bed him as it is to jerk off. A guy like Joe will teach you what jealousy means.

"Just know that they aren't going to say no," he says of his sexual conquests. He is mentoring me, though he doesn't know it. I, too, will abandon guilt and consideration and I will not care about becoming a fuckup. I don't know why everyone wants to be so fulfilled but I've finally succumbed to it. I want to be led around by my dick. Fearlessly, like Joe.

Perry calls my cell phone all the time. I change my number but he calls everybody I know to find it and somehow it is leaked. I shouldn't be paying any attention to his messages, full of anguish and threats. He went from loving me to hating me pretty quickly. I should be reporting him to the police, or at least ignoring him. He is pouring his pain all over me, cramming it up every orifice, and I don't want to hear another word.

I tell Joe.

"The guy's being a jerk," he says. "Just erase those messages before they're played. You don't have to listen."

Now I am a nomad. I left Perry with everything except for a few prescription bottles I swiped on the way out. Besides that, I didn't take a single teacup. I can move around as much as I want now and I don't have to be accountable to anyone. There will be no fake trips to the library. I don't have a bed but I can sleep on the floor. I conk out easily with all the pills.

I couch surf for a bit, but then Joe invites me to stay with him and Alan until I figure things out. When he presents this opportunity we are sitting in the window seat of a diner on College. It's a rainy, foggy day.

"I don't know if that's a good idea," I say.

"Why not? Alan likes you."

"And I really like you," I say. "Too much."

"Is that all? We're young men," he says, like that will make up for anything. "We can work it out."

"Perry's already pretty angry," I say. "This might make things worse."

"Fuck Perry," says Joe. "You're free now." And he stands over the table and kisses me. Anyone could see.

I move in.

Joe and Alan often have friends visiting. They come to drop off a plant or stop in while they walk their pets. Barking dogs, revolving doors, extra people at dinner. New people. Some of them turn into dates. We meet for beer, then I bring them home. I'll think about Joe while we fool around and then I'll ship them off before anything big happens. Sometimes they say something disqualifying, like that I'm a great guy or that I'm sexy.

See? I always think, fantasizing that Joe would overhear. See?

After they leave, Joe will always come out of his bedroom to say that I seem agitated. "What's wrong?" he'll say softly, holding me. Alan is a deep sleeper. "Tell me what's wrong."

But he knows what's wrong so I say nothing. If he's horny we'll fuck, quickly and quietly. I'll take him from behind and he'll say oh yeah and I'll ask him if he likes it and he'll say fuck yeah. There are no other words. Then he'll pull up his pyjama bottoms and have a smoke at the window, inhaling with authority. A different kind of buzz for him, equally innocuous.

He never leaves town and hardly ever stays out late. He loves all three of us to eat together and he makes jokes about our family unit. Unless I'm at work there's no relief from him and even then he knows my schedule. The flights to the islands are packed this time of year and I'm grateful for it. Six drink orders at a time. Zen-like distraction. We get a lot of turbulence over the Atlantic, too. I get to feeling badly, so I go to the bathroom and force myself to throw up. Then I have a quick cry or I jerk off. Whatever brings relief. My cell phone rings as soon as I turn it on after landing.

"Come home," Joe says. "I've got your dinner ready."

I work a rare winter charter and get a day to myself in San Francisco. I wander around Fisherman's Wharf, and then I head on over to the Castro. Rainbow flags and lattes. Old fags nursing pitchers of stale beer. It's the same as everywhere so I take a street-car to Haight-Ashbury and walk up the steps of Buena Vista Park. I'm not sure what I'm looking for but it's really hot so I sneak behind a bush and take off my pants to move my underwear into my pocket. As I step out from the greenery, I see a guy. He's tall and muscular and droopy-eyed and he gives me that look that is becoming unmistakable. My legs shake the whole time he's blowing me. It's broad daylight and I don't normally do this kind of thing. Not that I think there's anything wrong with it.

"Thanks," I say.

I reluctantly tell Joe. He really does draw it out of me. I didn't want to tell him because it felt disloyal. He gets more and more excited throughout the story, though, and when I'm finished, he stands up and claps.

"Bravo!" he says. "Well done!"

I think of Perry and the way I left, the mess he's probably in. He's stopped calling me and I'm afraid to call him. When we were together, at least somebody was happy some of the time. He'd make me lead him around the living room when I pulled a mood while Ethel Merman plugged away on the stereo. He'd force me to dip him and then he'd bounce back up with such flair. No matter what season it was, Christmas lights twinkled around the apartment. Despite everything, I'd often find myself suppressing a smile.

One wall yellow, one green, one brown. Then I'd come home and he'd be painting the white one pink. Or reconfiguring the speakers. Or hanging something on the wall that he'd picked up off the street.

"Where did you get that?" I'd ask.

"Somebody's garbage," he'd say. "Can you tell me why on earth somebody would throw out a perfectly good mirror?'

Alan brings home the colours test from his human resources development day. Alan is a blue: reliable, dogmatic, punctual, hard-working. Joe tries it and he's an off-the-charts gold: spontaneous, sociable, impetuous. I sit at the kitchen table, filling it out while they make dinner. I know where the questions are leading—I'm going to end up a blue. But I don't want to be a blue, I want to be a gold, like Joe. There's no use making up the answers so I rip up the test.

"This is bullshit," I say. I do not want confirmation of anything.

It's a cold and bright Sunday. Even after all this time, it's still winter. Joe and I get on our bikes while Alan stays home to watch a movie.

Joe is the craziest cyclist ever. He leads the way and somehow I keep up. Hero worship. Our tires crunch on the ice as we jump all the tracks and then breeze through the tunnels by Union Station, run our bikes up the stairs and careen along the Skywalk, horrifying the pedestrians. Then we jump the steps all the way down to Queen's Quay, go back uptown through the deserted skyscraper courtyards, winter road sand spitting off our tires. He makes me take risks I never thought I'd take. We race down University Avenue, empty on the weekend, eight lanes to ourselves, sun speed and wind, I am high on him.

When we return, pink-cheeked and frosty-eyelashed, Alan has finished a load of laundry. We don't have a dryer so we hang the wet clothes all over the house and turn up the heat and the fans. The house has a distinctive smell—fabric softener, sex, male sweat. You can smell it as soon as you walk in the door. It's a smell I'm beginning to love and hate. It sends my vitals off the charts. Just like the music that is always blasting, Neil Young and Dylan, I'm already nostalgic for it. There's always something happening here—Alan's making a pie or starting seeds for the garden, Joe's building shelves or burning CDs. We have a huge communal canvas on one wall. It probably has a hundred layers of paint. I'm not an artist but I like to make words. I squeeze out some silver and dip my brush in it. *Everything I say is a lie*, I write.

46

"Whoo," says Alan. "What a cryptic mystic."

Then he kisses Joe and tells him he needs a hot shower and Joe laughs and they go off into the bathroom together. The lock clicks. I lie on the couch and try to watch television but the walls are too green and I can never concentrate.

After Alan goes to bed, Joe and I decide to go out dancing. He puts on a sleeveless basketball jersey that no one else could get away with.

"How does this look?" he asks, but then he half-smiles. We both know there's no point in asking me.

We hit the club, take some ecstasy. Joe likes to talk when he's this high, have a heart-to-heart. He pulls me into a corner, locks his crystal blue eyes onto mine.

"Thank you," he says, "for making my life more interesting."

Perry's there, too. For a second I freeze. But after he recognizes us, he ignores us. He hasn't spoken to Joe since he and Alan took me in. Perry's with a cuter, more muscular version of me. The guy can't keep his hands off Perry, who looks smug, despite the new lines that are etched on his face. I watch for a bit and turn away. Relief. Someone else is looking after him.

We leave soon after that and walk down to the water to watch the sun come up. We grab steaming hot lattes from our favourite spot in Kensington and then get back just as Alan is leaving for work. He clucks disapprovingly but chuckles, too, like we're some rowdy but good-hearted teenagers. The sun is streaming in and there are no blinds, so, after Alan leaves, Joe takes a yellow sheet and nails it over the window. Everything golden. We fuck in the glow and then lie in bed, intertwined. We're still allowed to lounge around in his and Alan's bed when we're stoned.

When we do it again I have to bite my lip. I feel too close to telling him I love him, like the words might just spill out. I should be enjoying this. I thought it was all I wanted.

I hold Joe while he sleeps, satiated and oblivious. His lungs rattle.

I look into his closed eyes and I know I'll have to go.

People sense sadness and stay away from it like it's a sickness. You can pick it up like that on a person. I run into an old friend who has a baby and she chats with me for a while, but then I see the click of realization and she holds her baby closer and says goodbye. I don't blame her.

I'm taking a breather in a deserted café at Yonge and Davenport. It's a rainy gray day in early spring. The trees haven't budded yet—it's no-man's land. Joe's on a job, Alan's at work, and I've spent the day looking at apartments. I was thinking about getting a little studio, a bachelor pad, even though I've never been a swinging bachelor. You can't be swinging and needy at the same time.

I've forgotten to eat all day again. The café owner brings me my soup as I circle a few more ads in the classifieds.

I haven't seen anything I like. I think about the dark and musty basements and renovated granny suites where every appliance and countertop comes from a fire sale. The dirty old high-rises with their parquet floors and laminate closet doors. Cheap windows installed fifty years ago. All of them echoing empty. No communal art or friends, no laundry hanging off the doors. No Joe.

I can feel tears start as the guy puts the soup in front of me. I stare at it and start crying for real and I curl up in my chair against the wall, not looking up. It's funny, I've been convinced that crying's something private, but when the owner comes back with my sandwich I am glad to have a witness. See me being sad. I never get to show it.

"We're not busy here," says the owner. I can sense him trying to catch my eye. "You can come and sit here anytime you want."

***

I give my notice to Alan and Joe. Joe is mystified and put off. "I thought you liked it here," he says. "I don't want you to go."

"I need to get the hell away from you," I finally say. He tries to look hurt.

Alan says he wants me to stay, too. I think he liked the way I kept Joe busy, out of Alan's way when he just wanted to read or watch television. He's another one I can't look in the eye.

I move into my new place, a square studio with one wall of windows. Nothing to see outside, though—just a parking lot and the entrance to a hospital. White walls and grey broadloom. I buy a futon and grey sheets to match the floor. A white chair, a few dishes, and I'm done. Nothing on the walls. I start to like it.

Alan comes by after work one day. He's picked up a plant. It's sprouting red flowers and I'll throw it out after he leaves. He looks around and tsks.

"You'll have to think of a colour," he says. I'm wondering why he even stopped by. He must think we're comrades.

"I'm happy with the way it is," I say.

Mostly I keep to myself now, but sometimes I look at a guy with a new certainty. It'll always play out the same way: we'll go back to my apartment, and he'll comment on the starkness of the decor and I'll ignore the comment. Afterwards, we'll lie on the futon and his will face hover over mine.

"I just know there's more to you than these blank white walls," he'll say.

I'll tell him for now there isn't.

YOU ARE NOT GOING TO LOVE EVERYBODY

EVERYBODY IS READING that flat belly book. Apparently we are all allergic to wheat. I had that Fulbright scholar over for a drink because at the Halloween party I'd been an angel and he'd been a devil but we didn't get up to much. He was American and good-looking and asexual. His field was obesity research.

I said, "It's not as simple as calories in, calories out, is it?"

He said no.

I was telling this to Jonas, my lanky quaffing buddy. Jonas lifted his pint, elbow still on the table. A big lump of tricep slid into place and I knew I was going to be in trouble. Towards the end of my annual Christmas party for stoners I accosted him in my kitchen and slid my hands right up under his shirt. He had been eyeing me all night. Little presents. I said do you wanna stay on awhile longer and he said are you asking me to stay longer and I said yes.

The last guest left and we made stealth movements in the hall, a little back and forth dance. I was wearing my lucky red tank and only the coloured lights were on. I had been wondering about that body. It looked a little haggard but underneath it was all power. This guy is an ageing lion. We kissed a long drawn-out slow one. Then our clothes were off and M83 was blasting and we were dancing close and naked and I thought we are going to fuck, we are going to laugh and fuck and talk and fuck and stretch and fuck and smoke more and fuck and exalt ourselves naked on the freezing cold balcony and it will all be to music, and then we did all those things. At the end of the night he sat shaking, naked and overstoned on the couch and I held him and said don't worry, we are brothers. I helped him dress and he went home to his boyfriend and the next morning I was a wreck, worried that it would never happen again and wondering why nobody ever told me this.

This has been going on for awhile. One night he brings E and he decides that we will go out. I am careful with him, affable. I take off my shirt on the dance floor just like everyone else. I grind with a lot of guys and in the toilet stall while Jonas is feeding me the second pill from his tongue there is some barely legal guy sucking my dick.

"He likes you," says Jonas. "You should bring him home."

"Not tonight," I say.

I go back to my place but don't sleep. I go through all my porn sites. I take out my toys and lube myself up and suck up my poppers and fuck myself and the physical sensation is incredible and not really any type of relief at all, even after I come. So I clean up the apartment and go to the all-night grocery store and stock up because I haven't really shopped for food since my Christmas party two months ago.

At daybreak I sob it out. It is not a relief either. I fall asleep until midafternoon and then go to my eye appointment.

I tell the optometrist that lately everything seems blurred.

He says, "Let's have a look and see."

He turns the lights down. He is tall and plump and Indian. He has a large staff and they sell a lot of eyewear. I forgive myself for guessing that he supports a big family with skinny sons who jump all over him when he walks in the door.

"Just rest your chin here," he says. "And your forehead here. Tell me if you are not comfortable."

I see a pretty red house in a green field. Yellow sun, blue sky. Delineated borders between the watercolours. Out of focus, in focus.

Out of focus.

"I am just going to have a good look in your eyes," he says. "You can blink as much as you want. Look back here, yes. At me. Here."

His knees rest against mine.

He says, "Your eyes are dry. You are not producing enough tears."

I say, really.

He says, "You should be using these four times a day," and he hands me a plastic vial. "Just a drop or two in each eye. You have to take good care of your eyes. Now you come back in a few weeks and we will take another look and you can let me know how you are doing."

After the appointment I go for a run. I run so hard. I take the ravines and trails because I don't want to stop at any streetlights and I don't want people in my way. I downloaded the music Jonas likes. I turn the volume up to full and it will wreck my ears and I have lost fifteen pounds since this all started. My face looks a little gaunt but I am cut. Before puberty I was a bit chubby. My brothers and sisters were lean so the Tab cola my mother bought was just for me, my special treat. Such intentions. When I run the tears come fast and quick. I had been coasting.

Jonas comes over that night and we smoke up. I used to just have a few tokes but now we usually smoke a joint and then I get up and roll another. I am becoming an expert. I grind the buds between the pads of my thumb and index finger and sprinkle the pot over the delicate translucent paper.

I look down at the paper while I am rolling. I ask him if he's had dinner.

He says yes.

I moisten the edge of the paper with my tongue and pinch both ends and roll a nice firm fat spliff.

"I really like you," I say. I light up and inhale.

"I really like getting fucked up with you," he says while I am handing it over.

I should tell him to fuck off but it is way too late. He lets me feel him up and we jerk off but he doesn't want to have sex tonight. So we go to the bar and get wasted. Tequila shots with the go-go dancers. We run into my yoga teacher who wants coke. Jonas leaves for a few minutes and comes back with the dealer. We all go out to the alley behind the bar.

"I'm trying to lose weight," says my yoga instructor. He takes the satchel and empties a small mound onto the space between his thumb and index finger and takes a huge snort.

My yoga instructor's name is Bill. He is my go-to guy. I go to class and Bill talks about good times and bad times coming and going, round and round in circles.

"You are not going to love everybody," he says. "And not everybody is going to love you."

In shivanyasa he rubs my temples, ever so gently, and my body shudders.

Jonas and the coke dealer have gone missing, so Bill comes over to my place to chill out.

"I really want to kiss you," says Bill. "But then I can't be your teacher."

I give him a blowjob instead. It takes a long time because of the coke. But I have lots of energy because I snorted, too. I would rather be running though. I wish I was on the trails, kickin' it and screaming. After Bill comes he says, "regarding me being your teacher—a blowjob has sort of the same consequence as kissing."

"That's not what any of my other teachers said."

My ex-yoga instructor leaves.

Jonas texts me in the morning. He spent the night with the coke dealer and used me as an excuse for his boyfriend.

If you are talking to him, just tell him I crashed last night on your couch.

He leaves another message a few minutes later.

It's not really fair to you.

I run again. I run every day now. For years my knee was sore and it hurt my lower back but miraculously my body is letting me do it again. My body is letting me run and run and run but it will not allow much food to pass through and it cringes a lot. At home it folds over itself and releases a lot of tears and I just let it.

I need more pot so I go over to Kensington Market to visit my dealer, who is also my fuck buddy. I know it seems like there are a lot of guys to keep track of here. But there is only Jonas. Everybody else is nobody.

Everything with the fuck buddy is easy. He lives alone on the top floor of a rundown house. I fuck him very hard and after I cry some more.

"Get a grip on yourself," he says.

He slaps on a pair of boxers and marches over to his special drawer. The drawer is sticky and he has to shake it open.

"How much do you want? A whole ounce this time? You've been really going at it lately, eh?"

My fuck buddy has a beautiful body and is charming but he doesn't have much else. We aren't really friends but the sex, for years, has been fantastic. He has a crystal habit.

"Let me try some of *that*," I say.

"No way. I am not going to be the guy who gets you hooked on meth. What the hell is the matter with you?"

I shrug.

"Man," my fuck buddy says, "I feel sorry for this Jonas guy if he's gonna have to deal with you like...*this*."

But Jonas doesn't need to worry. After the initial admission I clammed up. My eyes probably give something away, but I will not be unpleasant. When he comes over I cut the lime for the gin and tonic and roll another joint and we crank tunes and get naked and play with the theraball and make out and if I get lucky we might go all the way. Then he goes home to his boyfriend.

I go back to the optometrist.

"Hm, I see a lot of redness. But your eyes seem healthy otherwise. Try cleaning them with baby shampoo. Don't worry, we will get on top of this."

One good thing that has happened now is that I am very lean. I am not one of those fags who worships fashion models but Kate Moss said nothing tastes as good as skinny feels and I am inclined to agree. I am hardly ever hungry, but if I am, I look Jonas up on facebook. Playing with his nephew. Showing off his medal after his team won the hockey tournament. Hiking with the boyfriend—so hot with the camping scruff. There they are in Maui, looking into each other's eyes at sunset. The boyfriend is extremely handsome and earnest. My stomach roils at the sight of it, but my blood boils, so I lace up and hit the trails. The music blares and the few people I pass I ignore. I am sweat-soaked and on the loose.

After, I go for a stretch and sauna at the Y. This guy Brad in the locker room says, "Whoa man, you are looking fine...nice six-pack."

"Thanks," I say. "I've been *running!*"

SHE DOESN'T WANT YOU TO HAVE A HARD LIFE

WHEN I WAS EIGHTEEN and came out to my mother she just wept and I was so hurt and confused because I thought she'd loved me unconditionally. Later she said, "Oh honey, of course I do, did you really think I didn't? I just didn't want you to have a hard life." And I think I have so much love to give but can you imagine how she feels? To be that crushed, that someone you care for might be *lonely*. And my life's been full of sex and dancing and nobody ever looks into my eyes when he's fucking me and I kiss about one guy a year and I get it now.

When I'm on a plane I pee in the sink. I'm tall and have a bad back and the cumulative effects of scrunching my neck and stooping against the curved fuselage to reach the toilet is too much. Have you heard of the drip, drip effect? It doesn't seem bad but then one day the floor collapses from underneath you. I used to jerk off in public washrooms all the time but now I prefer to come in a guy's face. I had stopped masturbating altogether for a while though; I had had this sadness and terrible sorrow that burned through my body and made me cry a lot. It was the end-tailings of falling for some guy I was sleeping with who had a boyfriend and he said he got scared and I have to honour that!

After the dude with the boyfriend and I parted ways, I swore off attached men. But then one sun-stained evening, stoned and glowing and calm on the ferry back from Hanlan's, I met Dillon. He has this chiselled body and golden skin and it was a rush to stare him down. When we got off the boat I said do you want to come over and hang and he said he couldn't get away tonight and that's when I knew I was going to be breaking my new rule.

We exchanged numbers and he said he had an understanding but I knew it wasn't as open as he made it out to be...

I'm into daytime fun, he texted.

So he comes over sometimes in the morning. Do they not need him at his office? He must have a lot of minions. He parks his Volvo in the visitor space and heads on up and when I'm fucking him he says you can do anything you want. You can fill and stretch my holes and send me out wrecked.

Dillon doesn't kiss either but in my empty grimy bathtub I pee all over his kneeling body and he looks up at me with clear-eyed submission. I cup the back of his head with my hand and stare back and this is our connection. I think of my mother. She was worried that I wouldn't be loved and I've got the best of friends but it isn't always enough. I want a good man to hold me; I don't want to be slapping around some expensively moisturized banker. This will be the last time, Mom. The last time. I was short on rent last month and asked Dillon for a quick loan and he said that would be a bad idea. But I bet if I shoved my ass in his face and shit down his mouth he'd swallow it like raw oysters.

When I fuck him we don't use condoms. I've had it with that kind of protection. Skin-to-skin, cock shaft against his dark and squishy insides. I use my spit for lube. Are you gonna mark me, he says, and I say yeah sure. If I was sick and horked into his ass the snot would make my dick slide even better and he'd love it.

After he leaves I smoke up and make pancakes and in the cupboard where I keep my overly-organic bran flakes some whitish larvae has eaten through the plastic and squirmy creatures are crawling all over. I throw out the sugar, the cheap spices, the Mexican vanilla. I get rid of everything. I coat the shelf in a blanket of Comet and scrub it out, and then I do it again. I slaughter every last maggot. Some fall to the black counter and start writhing away and I have to get those ones, too. I have to kill them all.

I'm glad Dillon didn't see that.

I saw him at that big gay Christmas party at the Carlu with his A-list posse; he smiled hello with those white, white teeth but looked so scared in his velvet dinner jacket. I have friends who are professors and doctors, I wanted to say. I'm allowed to say hi. But we're all old enough now; I get it. All these guys have co-signed on mortgages. They have wine-tasting cruises booked and paid for and five-hundred dollar tickets for gala fundraisers and they don't want any upheaval and anyway there's other guys who can take my place and it's easier than figuring out who gets to keep the cottage.

A few weeks after the Carlu I am at an afternoon open house hosted by nice well-intentioned friends. There are some cute guys here but I am hung over and having trouble moving. I get stuck in a corner with this smug financial comptroller guy. Rakish and polished. Tailored dress shirt and tight-fitting cashmere V-neck.

First thing he says is, that's my partner over there. He points vaguely across the room. I look around and see a guy who looks like Dillon but I'm not sure. He's gym-built, with a conservative haircut, nice bleached smile, and pointy shoes but there's a dozen guys here fitting that description and *I really don't fucking know.*

Do you have a boyfriend? asks the guy.

No, I say.

Why not?

Because I'm the guy who pisses on *your* boyfriend when you're at work, I say. And he looks a little startled, but maybe that's because he can't tell if I'm speaking in generalizations.

TREAT YOURSELF TO THE VERY OCCASIONAL CIGARETTE

I WAS THE KID THAT PARENTS wanted their kids to hang around with, and it was no exception with Eamon Sweeney. We'd stay out late, whipping up and down Lakeside or smoking dope on the ski hill and his mother would never question anything. I wasn't inherently better behaved than anyone else—just more of a chickenshit.

I was caught up in Eamon's audacity. "You're too good," he'd tell me. "Say *fuck*."

"Fuck."

"Oooh, yeah. I like it when you say that."

He'd sidle up behind me in the locker room after soccer practice and push his crotch into my ass, dry-humping me while his newly muscled arms wrapped around my chest. Whispering stories about the girls he was banging. *You do it like this, from behind. It feels so good. I wonder why you haven't started.*

Now moan and tell me you want it.

I wouldn't play along with that, of course. But I wouldn't always snort and push him away immediately. Sometimes I'd be still and wait for him to stop, full boner under my tight underwear.

There was no context for this. There was no psychologist interpreting over my shoulder that Eamon was experimenting with his own power. It was just me, enthralled and only knowing enough to not let on.

I was over at the Sweeneys' place all the time. Eamon's father was never there but Mrs. Sweeney would make dinner for us and his sister Abby. Sometimes I'd be there even when Eamon wasn't. They had a jet-black Isuzu Rodeo with beige leather seats, and Mrs. Sweeney would send me on errands with it. Then she'd make coffee and we'd sit and tell jokes and she'd tell me about the guys she dated before she got married. Her favourite one dumped her and moved to Toronto and worked at Queen's Park for a while. I told her he must have regretted letting her go.

"Oh, I guess. I can only imagine what became of him."

I was just getting into working out then and Mrs. Sweeney was into Jane Fonda. Eamon and I were playing cribbage in the living room one day when Mrs. Sweeney walked in wearing her pink leotard. She pushed in her tape and started exercising.

Inhale up...and down. Warm up those arms!

"Mom! Gross," said Eamon, and he retreated to the kitchen to make toast. I got down on the creamy Berber carpet and did the moves. "Nice of you to join me," she breathed out, between reps. "Why are people so afraid to sweat?"

I picked up Eamon on graduation night, before we went to get our dates. His dad was home from work to mark the occasion and he handed each of us a Bud. I was wearing my dead grandfather's ill-fitting tux. My parents instilled me with love and comfort and not a whit of sartorial sophistication. Mrs. Sweeney must have noticed my white athletic socks.

She took pictures of me and Eamon arm-in-arm on the couch, drinking our beer.

"What a couple of handsome men," she said. She paused as she squinted into the viewer. "I bet you two will break some hearts tonight."

We headed off to the Best Western. The tickets cost twenty-five dollars and included, preposterously, lime sorbet after the soup.

This is what must have happened after we left Eamon's house: Mrs. Sweeney concluded that I simply could not spend my graduation night wearing gym socks. (She was the type of woman who bought a new Linda Lundstrom coat every winter and frosted her hair at the most expensive salon in town.) She raided her husband's dresser for some black dress socks and drove over to the hotel with Jenny. I remember Abby coming into the banquet hall and looking around, taking everything in. She was fourteen. She smiled and waved me over.

"My mom wanted you to wear these."

I wasn't embarrassed because I was so used to being taken care of. I stepped into the lobby and took off my shoes and changed while Mrs. Sweeney waited in the car.

After the dance we went to a party at Marnie Rodgers's big house on the water, where we experienced the usual drunken she-nanigans. I woke up in a twin bed, Eamon curled up in a ball on the floor beside me. He'd gotten so wasted the night before that he'd confessed to being a virgin.

We had the same crappy housepainting jobs that summer and continued to hang around together. But Mrs. Sweeney had turned.

Now she sounded irritated when I'd telephone for Eamon. And she stopped asking me to stay for dinner and overnight, though this went on anyway because Eamon didn't care what overtures she did or didn't make.

Sometimes I think about her waiting that night in her car, fingernails maybe making soft clicks on the steering wheel as she watched out for for Abby. Mrs. Sweeney was intelligent. She was a nurse because that had been the most prestigious profession available to her. What had she been thinking? She treated herself to a very occasional cigarette, so I suppose she might have been sitting there in a cloud of smoke. Was she remembering her own high school dances? I don't think she had a happy marriage. Not that I paid attention. I was too focussed on Eamon.

I've never been able to figure why she felt so compelled to bring me those socks. Possibly it was some maternal urge. Perhaps she just saw another human being in need of help. In any case, she must have figured out that I lusted after her son. After that night her narrow eyes would scrunch up with suspicion whenever she'd ask if I was dating a special girl yet. She'd become a sleuth. She worried like any mother. She looked after herself and exercised and had a tight, fit body but even in her mid-forties she was developing deep and terrible crows' feet.

Maybe from all that slit-eyed guesswork.

CHOOSE A DARE OVER A TRUTH

It's early evening on the last day of lifeguarding season on Lake Chippewa, and Lucy is dislodging the buoy lines from the underwater anchors. She likes to unclip them herself, although I undo the raft because I'm the only one who doesn't mind the weeds underneath. Vance, our favourite homeless patron, is helping. He stands on the raft, focussed and ready with the big chain opener. The other lifeguard, Gerry, is on the chair, trying to watch a mom wading with her daughter. The mom and daughter are sucking on giant red Freezies and showing each other their stained tongues. Gerry's head falls down gently, then snaps up, which annoys me. You have to watch, kids especially. Not just dream about it.

From up on the chair, I give Gerry a half-playful whack on the head, and then I jog out to the water and swim out to Lucy and Vance, being careful not to slip on any of the rotting slick boards as I haul myself up on the raft. Then Lucy heads back to land to retrieve the paddleboard so she can take Vance for a ride, and I put on my goggles and jump in with the chain opener. The weight of it takes me straight to the bottom of the lake, and I get right down amongst the scummy plants. I'm used to checking around under here, just to make sure everything's okay. I find the anchors, and unhook the chains. My air bubbles rise through the green murk, up to where Vance stands. He crosses his arms over his hairy belly and stands still as a Buddha, while he waits for Lucy.

When I surface I joke to Vance that he's now floating out to the middle of the lake and he grins. He's a little bit slow but he loves a joke. He's a good swimmer, too. Lucy parks expertly alongside the raft and shifts down to the rear of the board. Vance gets on in front. They lie down on their stomachs and paddle away for a final tour, over towards the marina.

They'll be passing by Lucy's father's boat. Lucy, Gerry and I took it out the other night with the lifeguards from the other beach. We were all drunk, Lucy was driving and she smashed and splintered one corner of the dock on the way out. We drove to the islands in the middle of the lake. Gerry and I lay at the bow, on top of the navigation light, blocking it to better see the stars and to avoid detection. We stared upwards and told lies about who we'd slept with this summer.

I put the chain-opener on top, and then kick eggbeater-style against the raft. It takes a while to reach the shallow water. Lucy and Vance pull in from their paddleboard tour and help me heave the raft up to the beach. I'll come back on Monday with the winter crew, we'll disassemble the raft and use the forklift to stack it by the guard shack.

The mom and kid have moved up to the playground, so Gerry has relocated to the bench inside the shack where he lies with the door open, watching in case anyone comes to swim. The buoy line is now only fastened to the two anchors at the waterline and in the breeze the once-square swimming area changes shape like an amoeba.

The reporter we've been expecting from the *Gleaner* arrives, his loafers making small cloud bursts in the sand. He introduces himself as Dan. He's been talking to our boss, who has sent him here to do a story about the end of town funding for beach staff. As the senior guard, I have to act as the spokesperson.

"How's the news business these days?"

"Pretty good gig if you like things slow," he says.

I hear the phone ring inside the shack. Gerry answers it without sitting up. Then he lazily aims the megaphone our way and mumbles that Luigi's will be here any minute. He lets his head fall back onto the flutterboards he's using as a pillow. I spread a towel out on the picnic table and ask Dan if he'd like to join us for pizza.

The five of us enjoy a light end-of-summer meal. Even the gulls don't hang out at the beach anymore, seeing as how few people come down each year with their food, so we eat in peace. We tell Dan that the people have stopped swimming here for many reasons. The new municipal pool up the road is one of them. It's a real crowd-pleaser—the roof is shaped like a wave. Tons of curved steel and glass. It nearly bankrupt the city.

"It's a stupid building," Vance says, with a touch of anger in his voice. It's a rare contribution to conversation, but he's showing his loyalty to us and the beach. "It's fake."

But people said the weather was too variable. We get thunderstorms in the summer and the parents want reliable activities for their kids. They said the lake water was too cold, but I don't think that's true. If I jog to the beach and dive right in, it's refreshing. If it's a hot day, the water warms up fast and gets almost too warm. If I'm tired, and have been moping around the shack, the water's a bit chilly when I first get in, but I always adjust.

Now Dan mentions the rising fecal coliform counts and Gerry scoffs. It's true the numbers are increasing, but the acceptable limits always vary depending on who's on city council. You can't see or smell anything bad and none of us have ever gotten sick. They publish the counts on the front page of the paper, though. Like it's a matter of life and death.

There are probably other reasons, though none are mentioned. Instead we tell Dan what a shame the budget cuts are, and how people never appreciate lifeguards when they're doing a good job, because no one ever sees what they prevent from happening.

"There hasn't been an incident at this beach for five years. We're trained to maintain a safe swimming environment. We're professionals," says Lucy. Vance snickers, but we make sure he gets the last slice of pizza anyway. Then he goes off for a swim while Gerry and Lucy and I start hauling in the lines. The buoys are the old-fashioned kind: eroded wooden blocks fastened together by rusted chain. Splinters come off in our hands, and the blocks get stuck in the sand as we haul them up the beach. The chains tangle as we stack them. Dan walks around us while we work, taking a few pictures in the peachy light.

I'm thinking about when we got to the islands the other night. We anchored the boat and played truth or dare. I always pick dare: kiss someone's nipple, suck somebody's toe, strip and swim naked around the boat. As the summer progresses, things get more outrageous—fluff yourself, pee into the water in front of everyone, light your fart with a match.

Gerry said to me, "Why don't you ever pick truth? I dare you."

"No loopholes," I said.

They are all younger than me, university students like I was before I dropped out. They all drink and smoke pot and nobody's a virgin. It would be inexcusable not to partake in everything on offer.

Dan interrupts our storage work. "Is that little dot way out there your friend Vance?"

We all turn to the water. At this time of day, the sun shines low to the west like a giant flashlight, making it hard to see, even with sunglasses.

"Yes," says Lucy. "I think it is."

"He looks awfully far out."

"Well," says Lucy, "there aren't any lines now to mark off the supervised swimming area." She walks over to the lifeguard chair and squints into the binoculars. She puts them down, but then looks again. Suddenly, she runs over to the paddleboard, yelling, "Greg, you be backup. Gerry you're third. I'm going out." Gerry goes up to the shack to retrieve equipment while I take my position at the chair, watching through the binoculars. Dan is beside me, and I can hear his camera clicking and whirring, clicking and whirring.

"What's happening?" he asks.

"You can see, here," I say. I hand him the binoculars. Vance is maybe a hundred metres away, but, because of the light, you can just make out his dark shape flailing in the shiny water. Everything scintillates. Every so often, Vance's head goes underwater for a few seconds. As Lucy approaches, his submerged time increases.

"Oh my God," says Dan, handing me back the binoculars and resuming his picture-taking.

Gerry arrives, lays out the blankets and opens up the resuscitation kit. Lucy has made it to Vance. She slides into the water and hooks his arms around the front of the board, then reaches over to pull Vance's legs on top, one at a time. She starts paddling him in. Even from the beach, with the shimmering light in our eyes, we can see that he's shivering and coughing.

"Shouldn't you be calling an ambulance?" says Dan, still shooting.

I tell him there's not much to worry about as long as Vance is conscious, and when they approach the shore I swim out to meet them. By the time I reach the board, Vance's eyes are closed.

"Can you hear me, Vance?" I speak loudly. "Can you hear me?"

He groans yes, somewhat dramatically.

"You're doing really good, buddy. Stay with us. We're almost there." I swim beside him until we get to the beach. Lucy and I drag him in and then she dries him off and wraps him in blankets, puts him in the recovery position while I assess his breathing and pulse and other vitals, yelling out my findings to Gerry, who records them on a Municipal Incident Report Form. Dan doesn't stop clicking.

"What happened, Vance?"

"Cramps."

"How do you feel now?"

"Saved!"

It's my first rescue.

After a while, when Vance is feeling better and lying warm, and Dan is still hovering over us taking pictures, I tell him I need his address and phone number so that we can file a report and do a follow-up.

"St. Andrew's United, tonight. If they have room."

"Oh sorry, I forgot. Well, don't worry, Vance, we'll take care of you." We get him into his clothes, and tell him we'll bring him to his shelter tonight.

Dan leaves soon after, not without telling us to check the paper the next day, which we do. *Dramatic Rescue Marks End of Swim Season* is the front-page headline, along with an overexposed shot of Jen heading out on the paddleboard and one of the three of us crowded around Vance. The editorial on page five is titled *Time to Reconsider Program Cuts*. It's the second time we've made headlines this summer, although it's only the first times our names have been used. *Rowdy Boaters Cause Minor Pier Damage* is the other.

We sit at the picnic table for a while, watching the sky change colour behind the clouds. The water looks blank without the raft and buoy line. It makes me uneasy. Gerry unscrews his coffee thermos and we sip our sparkling wine from rinsed-out Tim Horton's cups.

"Good job, Vance," I say.

"Excellent work, dude," says Gerry.

"Keep a lid on it, Vance," says Lucy. Then she hands him the thirty bucks we'd settled on as payment. I see the mom and her kid pass by. The kid must have spilled half of her Freezie onto her white swimsuit. She looks like a little butcher.

I work for the town in the off-season, too, as a maintenance technician for Parks. Mostly I just whitewash things and ride around in the truck. My colleagues are a bunch of friendly beige-toothed geezers. Not hearty old men with war stories. Just guys who started out doing what I'm doing and never left. Smoking non-stop all day except when we have to go into City Hall. Double-double with an éclair every coffee break. Budweisers and darts without fail after work. I rarely join them. They always call me Old Man.

Our boss is the same woman who manages the beaches. She came by the central shop today to talk. She had a talk with me five years ago, too. The police were there that day. They were doing an investigation into the drowning. Someone had said I'd been nodding off on the lifeguard chair. But the inquest determined that was hearsay, and that it had been impossible to see the water with any clarity at that time of day anyway, owing to the harsh glare. Besides, the girl had been hidden from sight, under the raft. When we pulled her out she was gone and blue. I tried resuscitating until the paramedics came, but it was too late.

Today, my boss told me that she'd had a strange call to the office, that a woman who had been down at the beach with her kid claimed that she'd seen us handing money over to the bather who had just been rescued. My boss wanted to know if I had any idea what that was about.

71

"I don't," I said. "Maybe she doesn't like lifeguards. Maybe she doesn't want her taxes going towards my salary and yours. But if you're concerned about it, you could always talk to the man whose life we saved, the guy who almost drowned. You know, you could let him tell you what happened himself."

"I can't do that," she said. "We don't have any contact information."

"Oh, sorry," I said. "That's right, he's of no fixed address." I waited for her to say something, but she didn't. "Well, it would be kinda hard to find him. And we can't pick on a homeless guy like that, anyway."

And she said, "No, I guess we can't," really slowly, and kept looking at me, but I didn't say anything else. So I think that's the end of it, at least until next summer, when we open up again. You have to keep the beaches safe. They're even buying rubber-and-rope buoy lines for next year, and a brand new raft.

.

NO MEANS YES

In my early twenties, my friend Peta and I worked in a boring country club bar with a guy named Jake, who wasn't overly friendly—just extremely sexy, which of course is enough. He had dark hair, permanent five-o'clock shadow and smooth, light olive skin. He was also a few years older than me, laughably macho and built like a brick shithouse. I knew he was straight but I was still attracted to him, mostly because I was stuck at my parents' rent-free place for the summer in buttfuck Northern Ontario and I had no one else to waste my hormones on. Not that I had been that successful in the city, but at least down there, there was the possibility.

Peta and Jake were very different. Four years in the Big Smoke and a year of grad school at McGill had made Peta relatively worldly, whereas Jake was just a foxy local yokel. He hadn't finished his first year at the local college and since then he'd drifted through joe jobs while living with his family and sleeping his way around town. Consequently, Peta thought Jake was a loser and Jake thought Peta was a snob. I wasn't really friends with him either but I think he respected me because I was okay at a few sports. I couldn't think past Jake's sex appeal except in the brief moments after jerking off, when I would realize he was an oppressor.

"Show us your tits," he'd say to a passing woman at our hangout. His admiring friends would guffaw appreciatively before going back to their pool game. "Remember, Jimmy," I overheard him slurring late at night to a buddy who was leaving with a conquest. "No means yes." I know he was joking, but it was the classic shit-for-brains stuff. That's the kind of sexy asshole he was.

Peta and I didn't get to work together much because we each had other jobs and we were always calling someone else to take our shifts. But when we did, I'd pick her up and we'd go in together. She was the first person I ever spoke dirty with. I spoke aloud about how I felt about Jake, and I loved it. I'd tell Peta what I'd do to Jake if I could. What I wanted him to do to me. We'd get hot and bothered and giggle. Jake would see us staring at him and look uncomfortable. It felt very right.

Towards the end of the summer, Peta and I went to a house party on the lake. We ambitiously brought along our two-four of Labatt 50 and stuffed our bottles into the master bedroom's ice-filled bathtub.

Everyone was there—people from work, people from high school, people I'd heard of but never met. And everybody was drunk. We skinny-dipped and played Twister with liquid dish soap. Lots of people went off into bedrooms and bushes. Everyone was mingling, laughing, being silly. It was a real knocker of a party, not the kind you read about in *Vanity Fair* or see in *Porky's* movies, but much better. And not like now when someone has to work in the morning or hasn't been well. We were all tanned and fit and drunk, and though we'd already all started off on our different paths, we were home for the summer and feeling forgiving and neighbourly and happy.

I was right in there with everyone else, partying away. Looking back, I guess it was a tough situation for a young gay guy to be in, stuck in some backwoods town, but people are always more hip than you think. A lot of people would tell me it was okay with them if I was gay, or they'd ask in a friendly way if it was a choice or was I born that way. It meant a lot at the time. It was a relief to be accepted for who I was. But those were bittersweet summers. I was so horny and unashamed, and it was wasted because there was no one to have sex with.

I was contemplating all this while I pissed away a few 50s into the toilet downstairs when Jake came in. It was normal to barge into bathrooms at parties. A lot of us were athletes. Nudity was no big deal. Jake said hello, unzipped, and started peeing with me, humming to himself. He crossed his line with mine. I honestly didn't look at his cock, which I'd learned to do by instinct. That's how gay teenagers survive the locker room. I laughed when our streams intersected, though. He smiled, and asked me if I was bored.

"Not tonight."

"But do you get bored sometimes?"

"Everybody does." I wasn't really paying attention. I was trying to finish up before I got hard.

"I get bored," Jake said. I'm sure you do, I thought. All you do is coast and fuck.

I finished peeing, shook and tucked myself in. I went to squeeze by Jake but he was already finished, blocking my way as he turned to me.

"What's it like for you?" he said. And he grabbed me in a gentle headlock and pulled me close. We just stayed like that for a few moments. I could feel his breath on my neck, smell him, the best smell ever. He rubbed his chin on my jaw, stubble, fantastic. He whispered something. It sounded like, "I'd like to know," but I couldn't be sure, and even then I wouldn't have known what it would have meant. It was intimate, yet threatening, like a test. I figured a safe thing to do would be to knee him in the groin, so I did and he let go.

"FUCKER!" he yelled, laughing. I smirked as I manoeuvred around him.

I went back out into the hall and Peta was following some people into a bedroom. I knew they were going to smoke up so I followed. One of Jake's buddies was yelling from downstairs for him to come arm-wrestle.

When you don't smoke up very often, you can suck a lot in when you actually do indulge. I coughed and coughed, and within minutes I was high as a kite. I was thinking about the headlock, allowing myself to wonder if there was more to it. I became pensive. Peta's friends went to go watch the arm-wrestling and Peta and I stayed on the bed. I told her about what Jake had said and done, and my feeling that he might have made a pass at me.

She didn't see it.

"You're right," I said quickly. "Just wishful thinking." It was strange though: I had never had the guts to interpret any behaviour by another man, no matter how overt, as a come-on.

Peta laughed and said that that's what dick logic must be, and suddenly I just felt drunk and high, and very lonely.

The three of us worked together the next night. We never got hung over in those days. We were still riding from the party, though the sense of festivity had mellowed into a pained giddiness. It was very busy, and I didn't get to talk with Peta much. That was okay, though. Vocalizing lewd fantastical plans for Jake just didn't seem right after what had happened. I was feeling some type of tenderness that didn't jibe with objectifying him.

Since it was so busy, all three of us stayed to clean up. Jake stacked the tables and chairs, Peta cleaned the bar and the dishwasher and I went to the back of the cooler with the big glass doors to restock the beer bottles. I liked to stack all the boxes beside me first, so I could just stand in one place while I put the bottles on the racks. I had just lined up my boxes and started replacing the first brand when I noticed Jake through the foggy glass doors, standing behind the bar with Peta. Intent on my task, I put it out of my mind, and soon I couldn't see them for all the brown bottles. When I finished, I put the boxes at the back of the cooler, and then stepped out, shivering.

I shouldn't have been shocked. I've always believed that you should kiss and sleep with whomever you want, whenever you want. But I have to say I was. Shocked. They were just standing there, looking at each other with lust, both sets of legs pressed into each other, hands on each other's hips and asses. They heard me and didn't step away. They just turned to me at the same time: a two-headed, multi-limbed creature, Jake looking like a sprinter who had just won a very minor and easy race, Peta blissfully and earnestly lustful.

"I'll drive Peta home tonight," Jake said. He turned around and walked down the hall that led to the parking lot. I didn't know what to say to Peta. I thought she hadn't liked him; it didn't make sense. I played it cool, though, said goodnight and winked, and she winked back without really seeing me, wide smile, eyes sparkling in anticipation of what would surely be a great fuck.

And all I could think was, next summer, I'm finding a goddamn job in the fucking big city.

YOU DON'T HAVE TO BELIEVE IN GOD, JUST HOPE

I'M STAYING IN VANCOUVER for the holidays again. It would have been nice to go away for once but I'm short on rent again and the catering gigs are too good to pass up. Tonight was a night-before-Christmas Eve fundraiser at the art gallery. Professors and developers, AIDS doctors and movie stars. I love it when it's busy and I slip through the crowd, silver salver like a halo, unseen. Some of the waiters do lines in the kitchen to help them focus and I watch them longingly but I don't do that stuff anymore.

Outside, it's pissing rain again. My skateboard hisses stealth-like through the shiny streets. It never snows at Christmas here, except for once, five years ago, when I was new. I went to Beaver Lake and missed my family. Fat wet flakes, as big as diamond pendants, floated down onto the trees. The ducks were angry.

I squelch along the dusty rose carpet in the lobby of our West End low-rise, past the browning potted fern and the gold-stencilled mirrors. I walk up the concrete stairwell and unlock the door, calling out to Jamie but he isn't home. He's the guy who lets me sleep on his couch for fifty bucks a week. He says he's a librarian but he keeps strange hours and doesn't seem to have any friends. I guess he's a lot like me. I'm awake as heck so I crack open a beer and flip through the channels. Lots of hot young girls are waiting to party, apparently. And there are a host of skin problems out there that can be fixed with complicated regimes.

I find *The Simpsons.*

"Every time you tell a lie, it makes the Baby Jesus cry," say the Flanders boys in their singsong voices. They are chastising Bart and I chuckle because the same episode was on last week and Jamie and I have been using it as a running gag ever since. Every time one of us does something bad, like smoke a cigarette or put a plastic bottle in the garbage instead of the recycling, the other one will say to not make the Baby Jesus cry.

At the gallery, after the crowd had thinned, I made out with one of the sous-chefs behind a garbage bin. Streetlights shone on his uniform so that he looked like an orange marshmallow. Carollers somewhere around us,

Come, they told me, pa rum pum pum pum...

I fumbled open a few of his jacket buttons.

A new born King to see, pa rum pum pum pum...

He struggled with my fly.

Our finest gifts we bring, pa rum pum pum pum...

"What would the Baby Jesus say if he could see us now?" I breathed into his ear. He buttoned his jacket up and said he had to get back.

A few beers later Jamie wanders in. It's four a.m. He's such a skinny guy that he looks sick. Maybe he is. He says he's twenty-four, like me, but he's got flecks of grey hair and lines around his mouth like an apple doll.

"Merry fucking Christmas," I say.

"It's tomorrow," he says. "Besides, I hate Christmas."

"Lame," I say. "It is so cliché to hate Christmas. What would the Baby Jesus say if he heard that?" I get a smile.

He's rolling a joint in the kitchen. "I need to calm down."

"Busy at the library tonight?"

"Haha," he says. He's not going to tell me where he was, I guess. It doesn't matter. It's nice to have some company.

He passes me the joint and I take a hit.

"Seriously, man," I say, exhaling. "Christmas is cool. Jesus was born. He gave hope to the people." I still believe that, more than ever, even though I've given up on the rest. I wonder if my parents know that. It's what I always liked best about the Jesus story. You don't have to believe in God, just hope.

"Don't start on that shit."

"I'm just saying," I say.

"Christmas to me is fighting," says Jamie. "Mom sloshed out by the Christmas tree, ice cubes jingling in her empty glass. *Be Mommy's special elf and get me another.* Then she'd pass out and throw up on the carpet. In the morning it would stink and Dad would make us be quiet while we opened our presents."

"That sucks."

"Anyway, that's why I don't celebrate it. Too many unhappy memories. I like it to just be over with so I can relax."

Which is sad, I think. I like Christmas myself. I enjoy the lights and the candles and the paper snowflakes in the windows. And the story. I remember the smell of bacon and Dad laying down newspapers for the new puppy one year. That really happens. At breakfast they always told my brothers and me that we were the most important gifts of all. They said that Jesus loved us no matter what, and so did they.

When I was seventeen, my older brother got married a couple of days before Christmas. His wife is a kindergarten teacher and they wanted to take their honeymoon during the school break. After the rehearsal I play-wrestled in the church rec room with the Best Man. He was twenty-five and on the rugby team. Something felt new and wrong.

The next day, at the ceremony, the minister had all the married couples stand up and we clapped.

Marriage is between a man and a woman, he said. Suddenly I knew everything.

"What's wrong, son?" said my Dad. He put his arm around my shoulders but I pushed it away because all at once I hated him. He'd made me and I could never be like him.

"I'm fine," I said, my new catch-all. But I was ready to test them now, to see if they'd meant what they said about Jesus. I didn't pass any more grades after that but I smashed a lot of windows, saw a lot of white lines. Oh yes Dad, I'm fine, fine, fine. It was almost a relief when the time came when I should have finished high school. They sat me down and told me I had to shape up or leave. I hitched straight to Vancouver. Since then we exchange emails and they send me cookies and toques and birthday cards. But I haven't spoken to them.

The pot and beer have got me wired. I find my raincoat and throw Jamie's at him.

"Put this on," I say. "We're going for a walk."

"No fucking way," he says. He's sitting on the couch, facing the screen.

"Don't make the Baby Jesus cry," I say.

I dress him, stuff his hands in the sleeves like he's a rag doll. He's all passive so it's easy. I haul him up, push him by the back towards the door.

"Where are we going?"

"Not sure yet."

And we head out.

Second Beach Pool. The bars on the fence make it a fortress, and the empty cement walls cast a white hue. We climb the fence and walk around by the shallow kiddie area. It's slippery because of the rain and we run along the deck and sit and slide when we get to the grade. We get back up and do it again. We're soaking and Jamie is laughing.

Dad would take us sliding in the winter and my sister and I would scream, ecstatically. The hills he chose were probably much too steep and there has never been anything as good.

At night, after hot chocolate, he'd tuck us in and I'd say let's go tomorrow again, Dad. It seems almost farcical, but we did those things.

I watch Jamie, sliding in the night. And then I hear a crying.

"Jamie! Listen."

He stops and cocks his head, and starts walking towards the sound. It's coming from some bushes that lead into the forest.

We kneel down and look in. I only see eyes at first, but then I can make out its wet, grey outline. Jamie reaches in and grabs it, so tenderly that I'm surprised.

"I think God would want us to take care of it," says Jamie and I look over to see if he's joking. We take it home and dry it off and give it a can of tuna and some water. The sun starts to come up as we drift off in front of another Simpsons episode on the couch. The cat rests on Jamie's chest.

The last thing I think before I fall asleep is that I could call my parents tomorrow to wish them a Merry Christmas. I could let them know how I'm doing.

I know they wonder.

OPEN YOUR HEART, IF YOU HAVE ONE

I MOVED IN WITH JARED after my apartment got sold because his old roommate was a homophobe and Jared kicked him out. I can afford my own place but it's nice to have company—fuck the complications. When I went over to check out his place it was obvious that we had a thing for each other. He brought me outside to catch the view from the eighteenth-floor balcony, and we both leaned over the concrete wall and looked out at the smoky frozen city, then at each other.

The place isn't fancy. The parquet floors are worn white, the cheap baseboards are falling off, and the light switches have been painted over so many times they're part of the wall. But it's comfortable, and the heat's included.

It's my first Friday night here. Jared makes a really good mac and cheese with bacon and onions and some other crap. We eat a bowlful each, slouched on the couch. Jared's not that good-looking but he's got these impossible ridges peeking out from the inch between his shirt and his jeans. They stretch down and in towards his crotch and I'd like to put my thumb on one and take it from there. Instead, I look the other way and we wash the meal down with shots of Jägermeister and swigs of Red Bull. You're supposed to put a shot of Jag into a pint glass of Red but we only have the shot glasses, so we just sip from the can.

"Technically, I'm your landlord," says Jared. "I should be supplying you with proper drinkware." He's not poor, but he usually just drinks bottled beer or take-out coffee.

"I know where we can get some pint glasses, actually," he says.

We don our parkas and go out. The snow squeaks under our sneakers and it's just the right temperature to be slippery as all fuck. I'm drunk and I love to sprint. The south side of the sidewalk on Jasper's been plowed and I just gun it, and for a few seconds I'm not out of shape, I've got no fat again, I'm just a guy with a six-pack and piston legs. Jared runs behind me, laughing and complaining.

"Stop it, man! Stop it. Follow me."

There's an old drunk staggering around a newspaper box, cradling his Tim Horton's cup full of pennies and nickels. He'll be a corpse tomorrow if the street outreach doesn't get him.

He says, "Open your heart if you have one."

And I say, "Sorry bud, good luck."

We pass that shit-assed tavern at 108th and there's a muscled hunk in a ribbed tank with blood running down his face. It looks like a red octopus has clamped onto his head, or a baby alien. Did someone bite his ear? He's texting on his iPhone. His friend is in the back of a cop car. The blue and red lights are flashing in the snow like it's Christmas but it's just another festive night at the straight club. You can feel the beat shaking the sidewalk.

Rihanna's asking *What's my name?* like any of the club sluts care. I love breeder dance clubs; you could get clobbered at any moment. They like to fight and we like to fuck, but either way, it's living.

"Just be respectful, man. Show respect!" The bleeding guy is yelling to his friend. He sounds like a jock in an indie movie, but it's real life. It's kind of alluring. We keep moving, though.

We sidle into the Delta and glide across the salt-stained lobby to the elevator, holding hands. The desk clerk watches enviously. You can't access the guest floors without slipping a key card into the number pad, but we go down to the lower lobby and find the stairs, which allow us onto the other floors. Someone could make a killing improving security in these places.

We wander the halls. I do a bit more sprinting. I try to walk the length of the corridor on my hands but can't make it. I check out the ice machine and stick a few cubes down Jared's back.

"I'm gonna get you for that," he says.

Everything in this place is a various shade of puke. But it's kind of luxurious. I stayed at this hotel once with a guy that picked me up at the old Roost. I guess *stayed* would be the wrong word. When we arrived at his room, I noticed that he'd left the bathtub filled with hot water.

"Why'd you do that?" I asked.

"The air is so *dry*," he sniffed, and I knew I wouldn't be hanging around after the sex.

"A-ha," says Jared, and he picks up two beer steins from a used room service tray that's sitting in the hall. It's full of dirty dishes and a small vase filled with buttercups.

"We need these, too." He pockets salt and pepper shakers.

We walk back to the apartment and wash out the beer steins and make proper J-bombs. I wish I'd taken the flowers, but they never would have survived the trip. We down our drinks, the shot glasses clinking against our teeth, and I turn on the radio and it's Pink. Lesbians love Pink. She's catchy. We dance the way we dance. I get down on the dusty floor and do some old dryland exercises from when I thought I was gonna be a champ. I can still lose the weight. I do an abs set and my stomach feels pretty tight, actually.

We pour another round.

"Cheers," I say, and I look at Jared and we drink up. I guess it'll happen now.

I take the steins and toss them over the balcony. Before they even land in the snow, we're kissing.

ANY SHOULDER WILL DO

IN OUR TINY PERFECT CLEAN room Beth hops out of her twin bed and leaves the white duvet askew. She draws open the curtains. She looks deep into her smartphone and applies her lipstick to leave a shiny scarlet island on her face. The lipstick is made from sieved french-fry oil. It costs thirty bucks and is marketed like cupcakes.

"It's really just to moisturize," she says. She runs her tongue around her lips. Then she looks at me charitably. "Do you want some? You're hangin' out of your boxers, by the way. Get up!"

We step forward into the bright early evening and traipse through the enchanting streets, navigating by the black brick spire with gold trim swirling around it like a Christmas ribbon. Christian Town. Were the earlier people proud to call it that, or obligated? The messages have gotten confused. Beth is a forty-year-old dentist who is holding out to meet some great man and get pregnant. I have a boyfriend who is a mumbling, irritating vibration. We bought a condo together a few years ago. He is not part of my life. Beth and I are backpacking around northern Europe, smoking a lot of dope and eating a lot of train station pastries. We can dine at nice restaurants whenever we want. This is another example of *confused*.

When I was packing Eric told me he hoped I would have a really relaxing time. That means, *I'm going to be sleeping around while you're gone so feel free yourself!* I haven't partaken, not for any other reason than I feel fatigued and doughy. Beth has been hooking up everywhere; she even finds men during our occasional gay bar forays. I keep losing her and then reconnecting in the mornings. She says she has to really be firm about condoms and that Scandinavians don't wash enough, but they have big dicks and are uninhibited. It's all as easy as sneezing.

Christiania is magically tucked away but we find it and enter through the colourful gates and march up to the bakery and ask for some cookies from the beautiful man behind the counter. He is about thirty-four, tall and thick and affable. One of those dark Danes. Maybe he even has an Arab grandparent. Looking so free of class-consciousness, looking so sexy and kind in his tank top and apron and hairnet. I notice myself staring. I turn away and when I look again he is smiling at me.

"You would like two cookies?" he asks us both. "That is all? What kind of cookies?"

"Uh...hash?" says Beth and the baker's eyes open bright. He laughs and says go to the stalls over there and they will help you.

"Have fun," he says. "Welcome to Christiania." He is eyeing pretty Beth. Then he sees me eyeing him and gives me a wink.

The *kiks* come in bags of three. "Start with a half," says the tough-guy vendor and we say okay and buy a joint to go with them. We walk by the band shell where some Swedish metal punk band is rocking out and head over to the water. It is forested and lush and the summer light is soft, soft and lemony-white. We each eat a strong-smelling cookie and then Beth says have the other one all to yourself so I do but of course they take time to kick in so we smoke the joint in the meantime.

We look at each other and think, are you as stoned as I am? The answer is yes. Beth says, let's go listen to the music. One of the haggards is selling hoppy homemade brew from a bicycle keg and we climb up the knoll with our pints to overlook the scene and everywhere are Danes swaying through hash smoke. Long and lean and fashionable, admiring themselves in each other's sunglasses. The music is fucking loud and I glance to my left and Beth is making out with some stranger and she'll meet me back at the hostel later. We go home in nine days.

I walk over to the art gallery that is at the top of an old stone army building away from the main action, and climb the graffiti'd stairs. It's one of those places where you feel like you're not supposed to be. Like you've gone the wrong way. The signs are only in Danish, obviously, and maybe I got mixed up and this is someone's type of communal home? But I keep going.

In the gallery the wide old floorboards creak and the only person here is the curator. He is fiftyish. He is wearing a loose, faded Tuborg t-shirt. Cargo shorts. Construction boots. He is lying on his back on an old church pew. There is a beige cat stealthing around. The space is shoddy but aesthetic and full of windows looking into the greenest clouds of treetops. In Toronto it would have been scooped up by a swooning yoga instructor. I stand there, hesitating, and the curator says something that sounds so foreign it is almost shocking.

I say, *undskyld.*

He says in English, "This exhibit is self-portraits of a trans-sexual artist. Some of them are not so good. Anyone who lives here can apply to show work. The decision is by consensus."

I amble around. The artist is female-to-male. Here he is lifting weights. Here he is fixing a car. Now he is smoking a cigar. I think there is nothing new about a transgressive transsexual. I think of the first time I looked at a big Cindy Sherman photograph. She was wearing an orange checked-cloth dress and lying down on that kitchen floor. It was obscene.

The curator goes back to his nap. Outside, the sky darkens in one blink and it starts to rain and when I notice how *yellow* the light is from the incandescent bulbs I realize that the cookies are kicking in too, heightening the high. I don't feel tired anymore. I feel a little more taut. I am going to have to be deliberate. I make a plan to finish looking at the exhibit and then to pick up a sandwich from the 7-11 and bring it back to the hostel and watch Danish TV or even BBC and maybe jerk off and try to sleep.

While I am still studying the pictures, a couple walks in, hand in hand. I don't look directly at them because I don't want them to see how stoned I am.

Some of the work is hard to see clearly because the finish is glossy and the light reflects back. The artist has tattoos, mostly of faces. All over his arms and chest. There is an unremarkable black-and-white of him standing naked. It's only a step up from a Craigslist personal. It is brave.

The couple and I are moving towards each other and I notice it's the baker with his girlfriend. He gives me a grin and I feel relief.

He says, "You are crying."

I had been feeling kind of asexual lately.

His girlfriend would make a model insecure. She acknowledges me in a Continental way and then disentangles her fingers from his and clicks across the space to stare at another photograph.

The baker is still a few paces from me but he is moving to me. Maybe he has always got to bang anyone he wanted to. That would create a different shape of person.

"Are you enjoying your time here?" he asks. He asks it gently.

I think I ate too many cookies, I start to say. Before I say it the baker has wrapped his arms around me and my cheek is resting on his chest. The girlfriend has noticed nonchalantly and she turns back to study the transsexual sitting stiff and regal on a horse. The curator sleeps and the cat has curled up on his belly. I close my eyes. I dislike time. I can hear the rain and the band in the background. The bass comes through the loudest.

Right now, though, in here, it is very, very quiet.

SOME PEOPLE ARE NOT HAPPY UNLESS

SUN RAYS STREAM THROUGH the windshield and glint off Rob's aviators and the dust in the air sparkles like fireflies. It is Sunday afternoon and I watch him shift gears expertly, slouched down, legs open. He's driving me, in his used Beemer, home from the gym. We'll stop for sushi on the way and get the specials. We've had everything from sea bream to aka-yagara to hoshigarei and the waiter knows to be boned up on what's available.

Sometimes Rob has a big dinner scheduled with his family after but he says he doesn't care. He grins over at me and says he wants sushi with his buddy on Sunday afternoons, damn them!

Inside the weight room the heaters burn through the mil-dewed sweat that emanates from the carpet. Top 40 music blares—Beyoné, Pink, Maroon 5—and we work out along to it but when we get in the car it's our own stuff—Sparkadia, The Black Keys, Radiohead.

We spot each other. I'm a hard gainer but I've made progress since we started working out together four years ago. We were always at the gym at the same time on Sundays and we always chatted so we thought why not. We have to adjust the weights in between each set because he's so much stronger—("FATTER!" he says, putting his flat palm on my stomach—"Why can't I have that?") but he doesn't seem to mind. He's not a muscle-head but he can bench 245. Three times. On the last rep he needs the tiniest bit of help, and I try to help him seamlessly, with no jolts.

The sweat drips down his face. He looks at me and says, you're the best spotter in here, bro. You know just how much to push, and I know you've got my back.

At dinner we talk. He wants the lucky details from my Saturday night.

We went dancing at that old warehouse at the waterfront. These young boyfriends were grinding me on either side and we went to the washroom to smoke up and they brought me into a stall and they took turns sucking my dick.

I went to Woody's. I ran into an old fuck buddy and we went back to his place and he made vodka sodas and then we just started tickling and wrestling and we didn't really have sex but it was still fun.

Thought I'd struck out. Even Easy Eddy was there, but he went home with one of my pals. Thought I'd walk home and jerk off in front of the computer but I ran into an old trick from Pride two years ago and he came over and we just started fucking right away.

The stories are fun to tell. I don't embellish and I don't hold back. Rob knows what rimming is now. He knows what goes on at bathhouses.

"Interesting," he says. "I wish us straights were more into this free love stuff. Man, would that be fun."

Then he'll ask his questions.

Did he come after you fingered him?

93

What happens if you spill the poppers?

Why did it smell bad? You mean guys need to DOUCHE?!?

One dinner I was especially glad to have him to talk to. I was in a funk. I had won five games in a row at the pool table at Woody's the night before. Then I walked right up to the chief stud and said we were going dancing and he should come with. His name was Alex. He danced mostly on his own, outside my group of friends, but always close by. He had moves. After hours I said there was plenty of beer at my house and the next thing I knew we were clinking Löwenbräus and kissing. Then more kissing and groping and a suggestion of lying down. I took his pants off and went for his ass and Alex chuckled confidently and said no and flipped me over. He got me ready pretty easily, slid right in. At the first break we sipped our beers and switched on some porn and smoked a joint and snorted a line and then things got perfect.

After we had let our minds drift he fucked me again. He kept me on my back and spit in my mouth and my whole body responded positively to that. Then we smoked some more. I went to take a leak and he followed me and told me to piss on him in my bathtub. Then I lay on the tile floor and he did the same to me. I felt so warm. The piss tasted tannic. Some people are not happy unless they are nearly passed out on a cold bathroom floor, ass dripping and gaping, mouth stretched, muscles sore, and covered in piss and lube and sweat and cum.

We took another short break. "How did you know I needed that?" I said.

"I just knew."

My hands were running all over his body. He had gone soft for a bit so I knelt down to take care of it.

"Mm," he said.

When he left I asked for his number.

He said, "Let's just leave it to chance and see what happens, stud."

I tell all this to Rob while we are munching down our edamame.

"I feel jarred," I say.

"I know it was raunchy," says Rob. "But at any point were you making love? Or was it just dirty sex?" His dark eyes watch me kindly. He is ten years older than me. He reminds me of my older brother except my older brother lives three provinces away with an Evangelical wife who thinks I need to be forgiven for my sins.

I say, "There is no difference."

Rob says quietly, "You are wrong. Even in your seedy little world. When you were fucking, were you looking into each other's eyes?"

But I couldn't remember.

Rob has kids. He had a son early on and now with his new wife he has two toddlers. The early son is a teenager and getting very surly.

"He is my special one," Rob says. "He is often moody and he yells at me and tells me he hates me and you know what? I tell him that's okay, I tell him if he needs somebody to hate it may as well be me because I love him and I will always be there for him. And then I tell him I am a stone castle and he can hurl whatever he needs to at me because I will stand strong for him.

"And sometimes he actually laughs when I say that, and he says sorry he's been acting rough lately and I say, 'it's okay. You're my son. You act rough around me if you need to.'

"I love being a dad," he continues. "I always knew I would. Besides, I had my own issues when I was a teenager."

I say, "I didn't know that. About what?"

"Oh, you know. Girls and...things."

He looks at me, and then takes a sip of his Asahi.

"It was a tough old town," he says. "That's why I got started on the weights."

After our bean paste ice cream, we get back in the car. The sun is just setting but the little sparkles are still there. He turns onto my street and downshifts and says oh man, ball and chain time. He has to shave during the week but by this point on a Sunday he's always stubbly.

Outside my building he idles the car, squeezes my leg.

"Have a good week, my friend."

Then he grabs my hand in a brotherly grip and brings it into his chest. I rest my hand on the back of his head and we hug.

"Don't let those hardcore fuckers get you down," he says. "Go find yourself a sweet guy like yourself."

Big grin. He still has his sunglasses on.

"See you next Sunday," he says.

I say sure thing. And then I get out.

EVERYBODY GETS MAN LOVE SOMETIMES

BRIAN OPENS HIS FRIDGE DOOR and pulls out two bottles. He twists off a cap and hands over a beer. Then he uncaps his own and we clink and sip and he looks right into me. I know that look.

His gaze alters when Jen comes in from the backyard, face flushed from gardening, and caresses her hand lightly on his beard. He smiles at her, blinks, and rests his hand on her hip. They've had a fight but it's over. Jen had found out about some concurrent dating that had been going on two years ago between Brian and this teller at the bank. Jen and Brian had been just starting up, so he had not seen it as an issue. Jen thought otherwise. But it seems to be resolved.

"You boys wanna go get the steaks for the barbecue?" asks Jen. She's at the sink with her back turned to us and she's waiting for the cold water to come through. I answer yes.

"You'd better get some more beer, too," she says. "The way you two drink." She makes a satisfied aaah sound after she downs the water. "I guess it's my fault, though." She turns to me and her eyes flash white and intelligent under her dark bangs. We went to the same parties in junior high. "Remember how I used to make those rainbow jars before dances?" She'd show up with a Mason jar full of contraband from her parents' liquor cabinet. A shot from each bottle and then she'd mix in some kool-aid powder. In the mornings we'd be sick, but proud to be hungover. Having fun was an accomplishment.

It's the same Jen that's so successful now. After her divorce, three years ago, she got a job in pharmaceutical sales and the doctors love her. She's very enthusiastic and she knows how to party. She takes them golfing and then out to dinner, and she can always find a live band. She's the top salesperson in Northern Ontario. They keep trying to get her to move to Toronto but she says she doesn't want to pull her five-year old, Adam, out of school. She says she's happy where she is.

Brian and I get in his truck and he finds some cigarettes. He hands me mine, filter facing, and when it's in my mouth he lights the match on his jeans and cups it with one hand. Not many people still know how to do that.

We're quiet, driving around. Sometimes there's tension, but usually things are just breezy and good.

"I'm glad Jen's okay about the bank teller," I say, and Brian agrees. I don't know what she was so upset about, anyway. When you get involved with the sexiest guy in town, you should expect trouble.

We stop at the butcher and I run in for the steaks. Emilio is at the counter. He's used to me coming in for three big slabs—Jen'll cut off a piece of hers for Adam.

"You say hi to Mr. Brian and tell him to take good care of that sweet woman and boy," he says, and I say sure and tell him I'll see him later.

I get back in the truck with the meat, tell Brian that Emi says hello, and we head for the beer store.

Brian and I met when I was sixteen and he was nineteen. I'm twenty-eight now. I was on the local swim team and he was an injured football player from the Catholic school. The day we first saw each other, he was doing rehab in the therapy pool and I was having the best workout of my life. I was practically swimming downhill and my kick was like the beat of a song. Two-hundred frees and I was moving faster than race pace, effortlessly. The numbers on the clock were surreal and Coach even gathered the younger age groupers around my lane for a look. Brian wanted to see what all the fuss was about so he came over to watch, too. On the last set, I touched the wall and looked up and he was standing over me. Smooth, taut skin over so much muscle. I couldn't concentrate during warm-down. I was in shock from the way I had been swimming, but mostly from looking at him. A beautiful man, hands on hips, looking down. It was seared into my brain. I hadn't even known that I was gay before that.

After, in the showers, steam and lather everywhere, cocks and balls dangling, he came over, all brown-eyed and earnest, and told me he couldn't stop watching me. I laughed out of nervousness and because it was a funny thing to say when you're both naked, but also because I was sure he was just talking about the swimming. I guess he had a bit of man love for me, even back then.

Brian parks at the beer store and we walk in to collect a two-four of Blue. He gooses me in the parking lot, says what a motherfucker of a day in this strange voice he sometimes uses where I can't tell if if he means the opposite. Inside, it smells sweet and nostalgic: A group of guys know Brian from poker night at Renaldo's Pub, where he's a regular champ. I never play myself, but they defer to me, Brian's buddy, tipping their ball caps and asking how's it going. Some type of nepotism. I can't say I don't like it. When we get to the cash, the tanned blonde at the counter nods hello and blushes.

"Hot day," says Brian in a friendly voice. She hands him his change and her hands linger on his for a moment.

"Have a good one," she mumbles. Brian chuckles and picks the case of beer up with one hand, light as a cereal box, and we walk back to the truck.

It was Brian who first told me about man love. This was on my nineteenth birthday, just the two of us. We talked about it over pool and pitchers, his treat. I was thrilled; I'd had no idea. He said man love is when you see another guy and he's so cool or suave or funny or athletic that you sort of fall for him.

But not in a sexual way, of course.

I said I get that, too. But I said for me it's different, because sometimes I'm not sure if I want the guy or I want to *be* the guy.

"Yeah," said Brian, his big hand taking a firm hold on the pool cue, girls noticing. Guys, too, in a different way. "That must be tough." And he smiled and looked in my eyes. His grin seemed more innocent then. He was handsome but kind of goofy and crazed-looking like he might be just about to dance naked on the bar or start a fight. He has these long black eyelashes, too, and sometimes they make him look so sad. I've always felt such kinship for him, along with everything else.

I wanted somebody to show me how to be a man. Brian took me to the basketball court. We'd play one-on-one and he taught me how to do a proper lay-up. He got me off the machines at the gym and showed me how to work with the dumbbells. His dad was kind of a religious-nut asshole but he'd shown Brian how to do some carpentry. We'd build tables and chairs in their tool shed and Brian would put his hand on my shoulder after and say well done, son, in this mockingly paternal way that would get us both chuckling. In the park on sunny afternoons we play fought, and I wasn't scared of him.

"We're lucky in the looks department, too," he said one night. "We can get who we want."

"Not me," I said.

"Don't worry," he said. He seemed surprised. "You'll find some lucky dude." But how would he know? He was just being a polite straight guy.

"As you know, things haven't been working out for me in that area," I said.

"I can't see why not," he said.

But it was my own fault. I didn't know where to look. It's not like now with the Internet and gay villages. We only heard that the homosexuals gathered by the highway truck-stop late at night, and sometimes behind Memorial Gardens. I didn't have the gumption to try going to those places, and somehow I knew I wouldn't find what I wanted anyway.

Brian and I return with the steaks and beer. We had a bottle each in the car on the way over. It's probably a dumb thing for a cop to do, but it's a small-town force and Brian is popular with the other officers. He'd probably wink his way out of it if we ever got pulled over. He'd ask them if they wanted to go fishing next week.

We got up to a lot of shit together after we'd first met—firecrackers in mailboxes, naked cliff-diving, four-hour drives to Sudbury to go drinking and dancing. We'd drop acid and go bowling, watching in awe as the ball oozed its way towards the pins. It was the beginning of the end of my swimming days but I didn't care. I had man love for him because he was such a hooligan but there was another kind of love there, too. One that I didn't want to think about. Brian fucked a lot of girls and when I told him I was gay he was more than supportive. I was seventeen and terrified. It wasn't a big city. It was the rural north and this was before it was an in-joke on every other sitcom.

"You're my best friend," he said, and he hugged me. That was more comfort than I had ever felt. He told me nobody would bug me as long as he was around. The danger was real then. You wouldn't get lynched or anything, but they'd beat you up if they found you behind the arena. Still, I maybe should have gone it alone.

Brian goes out to light up the grill and Adam, who is home from gymnastics, plays a video game in the living room. Jen and I make a salad in the kitchen and I chop up the onions while she gives me a synopsis of her latest feelings on the bank teller situation. She's resolved that it's in the past and it can't be changed.

I've always gotten along well with Brian's women. Except for Jen, though, I'd never been friends with any of them beforehand. Things changed a bit for me when they started dating. I hadn't seen Jen since high school and now I was her confidante. Sometimes, after a fight with him, she'll call and ask for advice, but I'm the last person who should be giving it. I never allude to his philandering with other women or anything else. I figure she enjoys sharing his bed at night. I know I would. Why ruin it for her?

The one before Jen always wanted to meet for lunch. Just the two of us. It was too much, the way she trusted me. Intimate sex details. Brian liked to do it up her ass and did she think that was strange.

"She speaks very highly of you," said Brian after. He seemed proud of me.

"I bet she wouldn't say that if she knew me better," I ventured. It was rare of me to even broach the topic. "If she knew how I felt about you."

Then he just seemed angry.

Brian comes in to get the steaks while Jen's talking about him. But he just retrieves them and disappears again out the back. When the meal's ready, the four of us sit down on the back patio. Brian and I drink our beer but Jen, uncharacteristically, doesn't partake. She pours a tiny bit of chardonnay into some soda water, and says that she's got a big presentation in the morning. Adam chatters on about the other kids in gymnastics while we enjoy the evening. The late-day sun streams through the trees and we are just friends enjoying a barbecue. The good-looking kid, the handsome couple and their bachelor friend. A magazine spread.

After dinner, Adam shows me some of his gymnastics moves and I try them out, too. I'm not very good but I can still walk on my hands, all the way around the backyard, and he claps. I let the change fall out of my pockets and he picks it up and I say if it's all right with his mom then he can keep it. Jen rolls her eyes and laughs and tells Adam he's lucky to have a friend like me. Then it's bedtime so I read Adam a story.

This is one I don't recognize from my own childhood. It's all about some weird migrating birds who can't find their way out of the forest. I do my best to give them each a distinct and funny voice. My Blue rests on Adam's dresser and I take a swig from it every few pages. I let him sneak a sip, too, and he looks up at me with a big grin, gratified to be in the beer-drinking club. Everybody gets man love sometimes.

"You're nicer than Brian," he says when the story's over. The birds were so all so hopeless that they decided to just stay put. I'm lying there with him, waiting until he falls asleep. Brian's tidying up the kitchen, right next to us, and I know he's heard.

"Well," I said. "I only see you once in a while, but Brian lives with you. It's hard to be nice to somebody all the time." We lie in the darkness.

After awhile, Brian comes in from the kitchen and asks if Adam's out yet. I look over and see that he is. I move to get out of the bed but Brian's hands are already under my armpits. He scoops me up and puts me down on the floor, all six feet of me.

"Let's play a game," he whispers.

The way Brian and I got closer was like this: I was twenty and still hadn't met a guy. No sex, nothing. Not that I hadn't been looking. We were at a summer party at a rich kid's place out on the lake and half the kids in town were there. We'd split some kegs and people had brought pot brownies and electric jello-shots. Everybody looked so hot. The house was huge and every room had people in it—playing cards or singing along to a guitar, making out or chilling out. Down at the dock, they were skinny-dipping and toasting marshmallows on the barbecue. The stereo was cranked.

In the rec room, I'd been having fun sitting in the hot tub with Brian and some other people. We were all cracking jokes. The girl beside me was this really tanned Ultimate player. She put her hand on my crotch.

"I've heard about you," she cooed. "I bet I could change you," and I felt the hot snap of sexual frustration; I got out of the tub and went outside. I'd swiped a roach and I sat on a log beside the empty guesthouse in the night air, the steam still rising off my body. I lit up and sucked and felt better and worse and then Brian was standing there. He didn't ask me what was wrong. He just sat down beside me and put my head on his chest and then we started kissing. That happened a few times that summer, and other times, later on. More than just kissing. And that shaped me, for sure. Something in me knew not to talk about it, not with Brian or anybody else. I knew to just take it when it came.

Since then, of course, there have been guys. You look at them the right way at the gym and they want to meet up after for coffee. Or we start to chat in a bookstore. Most of them are closet cases and some are married. The sex has always felt like jerking off. They come over to my apartment and stand at the window, looking out at the water.

"Nice view," they say, turning to face me.

"It's just the lake," I say.

"I wasn't talking about that," they'll say. But the joke's gotten old. I know there's something better.

* * *

When Brian and I come out to the living room, Jen's setting up Trivial Pursuit. I notice a bottle of champagne on the table and three glasses. Something teeters.

"Before we start," says Jen, "Brian and I have news." But I already know. Jen had told me they'd been trying. She's only two months along but they wanted me to know first.

"That's really great," I say. And it is. A family can be everything. "Congratulations. It's gonna be a lucky kid."

Brian pops the cork and fills his glass and mine. Jen, of course, only gets a drop. "And something else," she says, after we've raised our glasses. "Brian and I would like you to be the godfather."

I turn to Brian, who's looking solemn. I mutter something about it being an honour and sure, yes, of course, thank you. I promise to do my best.

Jen hugs me and kisses Brian, who hugs me in this fierce way he's always had, in public or private. I know people respect that about him.

We sit down and play. Names, nursery plans, what'll you say to Adam. It's all discussed. It's exciting, a new baby. It's good.

Jen really does have a presentation in the morning, and she has to get Adam to school. Brian and I have the day off. Before the game is over, Jen gives me another hug and kiss goodnight and tells us to enjoy the rest of the champagne.

Brian and I continue the game, but it's obvious neither of us are into it, so we turn on the TV instead. Often, when we're alone, he'll sit on the couch and I'll lie with my head in his lap, or vice versa. Nothing more than that, just peace. But tonight he stays in his chair, rigid, and stares at the screen.

After a bit, I get up to go. He follows me to the door.

"Congratulations again," I say. "It's a big step." He nods his head in agreement but his jaw is set.

He goes to hug me goodbye and he puts his hands right up under my shirt and around my back. He holds me for a really long time, longer than usual. I bury my face in his nape and smell him and it feels so good and it clears my head, but I know it'll only last a while.

BEING WITH YOU MAKES ME FEEL SO BAD

I SHOULDN'T BE GOING OVER THERE, but Ted sounds so sad. He's been arguing with Mel again, and she's gone to stay with her parents. I'm supposed to be a friend and I feel sorry for him, I think. But my motivations are always shifty.

When I cycle around the corner I see him standing in the doorway.

"Hey bud," he says.

"Hi," I say.

"Get in here."

"Okay."

I leave my bike in the foyer. Ted's whole place is ramshackle. When Mel moved in, I had wondered if she'd fix the place up but she's not the type. She's too busy training for her triathlons. The house has three bedrooms: one for Ted and Mel and the other two are full of bicycles and dumbbells and drying swimsuits and boxes of trophies.

Ted passes me a beer and we clink bottles and eye each other before swallowing.

Don't look at me like that.

After Ted fucked me the last time, after he told me he was thinking of making a fresh start and wanting to wake up beside me in the mornings, and after he changed his mind and said he enjoyed being a heterosexual, I had to take a break. I was lucky that I was at a big company with an HR department. I filled in the forms, I took a leave and went to California. I learned meditation techniques.

"Cravings," the teacher said. "Aversions."

When I came back to town I didn't call him. But we ran into each other at the gym. A big hug by the weight racks. That was a few months ago, and we've met up for the occasional pitcher and game of pool ever since. No sex, though. Just two pals hanging out.

"I can't do this anymore," I'd said, before I went west.

"I understand."

"I get so fucking lonely."

"I know."

"Being with you makes me feel so bad."

"I'm sorry."

I always give him all my information, but he divulges nothing. His eyes stay shaded under his ball cap.

I ask him what he's thinking.

"*Nada*, dude." Or else he'll say something about the show he's watching so intently on TV.

We sip our beer and decide to watch baseball, which is a farce because neither of us are fans. Sitting on the couch, it feels like our shins are touching and I sneak a peek but they're a few inches apart. It's only the energy.

The game finally ends and the news begins: More Soldiers Killed in Iraq! AIDS statistics. Massacres in Darfur. Ted always makes the first move. We kiss and I put my hand under his shirt and press it into that heroic chest. He lifts me by the armpits and I'm sitting in his lap, facing him. We make out in our familiar way. It's not as good as it was before, but it's Ted.

My shrink keeps an ad in the local pink pages. She wears skinny jeans and has frosted hair. She keeps diplomas and golf plaques on the wall and pictures of her kids on the desk and hot water in the pot next to a selection of teabags. Her golden lab curls up by a big-leafed plant. Behind her, the window offers up a lovely view of the old town and all those expensive houses.

"He's emotionally unavailable to you," she says.

That means I'm convenient.

Our shirts are off and his eyes are closed. He's thinking of Mel, or more likely some guy that he's too chicken to pursue. He's using me but I need his dick. I'm willing to overlook all the trauma this will cause because I can never get enough of him. I can't just spend life sitting in a chair. The atmospheres are warming.

I unzip him and suck. He's hard like a slab of stone.

Fuck me, he whispers. This has never happened. His hole is wet and soft, I'll slide right in. I lube myself with spit. I hear people screaming, ends of discussions. I watch myself enter and I come immediately.

I give a few thrusts and then I pull out and apologize. He just looks at me, pleadingly. It's obvious he wants something up there, so I put a bunch of fingers in and pummel away while he jerks off.

After he comes he gets up and goes and grabs a dirty towel.

"You were pretty quick off the mark there," he says while he wipes himself.

"It was a little weird," I say.

"You can't tell anyone about this," he says.

But I've always been discreet. We've been fooling around since we were teenagers, pushing each other off the dock and getting drunk at parties. One thing would sometimes lead to another. He fucked all the girls and me and it was a long time before I figured out how to meet other guys, and that was only after I came out.

Why do you have to tell them? he'd hissed. It was the only time he'd ever been mad at me. By then I'd imprinted on him, a Lorenzian gosling. Now we're thirty.

"Nobody can find out about this," Ted repeats.

"I fucking know, okay?"

"I'm just saying."

"Sure."

I leave. We've never had a sleepover. I bike along the river and bum a smoke off a wrinkled fisherman. He's as skinny as a breadstick. He's wearing a stained white tank and old pleated chinos.

"Catching much?"

He grunts and lights me up. I sit on the concrete bank, inhaling deep. I shouldn't have gone over there. It was a step back.

I bike around town until dawn and lie in bed looking up at the ceiling fan. It clicks and wobbles like it'll fly off any second. It could chop me to pieces. Fag tartare. Life is full of danger and everything is breakable. I doze off and wake up a few hours later, grey and tired, and I know I've started slipping. There are empty spaces before each thought. I open my eyes wider than usual but I see less.

I go to work and start making my calls. I'm a sales rep. My bosses think being gay makes me sociable with the clients, but the truth is that I know my stuff. I'm super-organized and I work hard because I don't really have anything else going on, but they'd have a hard time believing that. Because gay guys are so much fun, right?

When I took this job, I thought some of the guys working desk jobs here would be queer but I was wrong. I should have moved back to Toronto.

Ted calls through to my station.

"Whatsup?" he says.

"Nothing. I'm busy."

"Mel and I had lunch."

"Uh-huh."

"She's gonna move back in on the weekend. We're gonna to try to work things out."

More slippage. I'm supposed to say that's good, and wish him well but I'm sick of being that kind of guy.

"Don't call me anymore at work," I say, and hang up.

After my shift, I trounce this gynecologist that I always play squash with. We're usually a pretty even match but I kill her today, whacking one ball so hard it ricochets off her thigh. She never even saw it coming and I'm tired of being such a bitter asshole. I apologize and she shrugs it off, even though we both know there'll be an ugly bruise.

Mel calls me the next week to invite me for dinner, but I decline. Half an hour later, Ted is on the phone.

"She doesn't understand why you won't come," he says.

"Tell her I'm jealous. Tell her I want her boyfriend."

"Ha, ha."

"I'm serious."

"Please come."

"Fuck you."

"Please!"

"Alright, fuck. What time?"

I show up with a kick-ass bottle of Treana and Mel greets me at the door, looking fit and confident. She has tan lines on her temples. She's read about the wine in the vintages guide and is impressed. Ted's gone to the liquor store—one bottle of wine won't even get us through the appetizers. Mel sits me down at the kitchen table to show me the photos from the wedding they were at on the weekend. I peer at the picture of Ted in his blazer, looking gorgeous and smiling, with his arm around Mel. I've never noticed his crow's feet before. The image of the two of them sears itself in and I smile and check my rage. The TV is on in the living room, and I can hear Oprah, pontificating on how to be happy. I flipped her on last week and she was interviewing this queeny author who said that we all have so much healing to do and I laughed and laughed and laughed.

Ted walks in holding a big bag of clinking bottles. He's wearing an unbuttoned dress shirt over a tight little v-neck and I want it all off. Mel is saying how I've been a good friend to Ted, and she and Ted will always be there for me like I've been for them and fuck, yeah, Mel, life can sometimes be hard but at the same time it can be really good, eh? *Also, I'd love to fuck your boyfriend again, another crack at that ass. I promise this time I'll give him a great ride.*

It's a warm summer evening and we sit on the deck. The horizontal light shines through the trees and illuminates the dandelion floaties. After we've eaten we light up a joint and I get the giggles. It's been a while. We break out the scrabble board but nothing makes sense. I drop a tile and go to pick it up but I can't stop chuckling, because a tile is down. Tile down! I'd crash and die if I cycled home. Mel fetches a pillow and a musty duvet and puts me to bed on the couch. In a bit, Ted comes in to give me a kiss goodnight. I'm still giddy from the pot. I tell him I hate him and kiss him back.

In the morning I hear them having sex. Ted comes out first to start the coffee and Mel follows about fifteen minutes later. I'm thinking about all the jobs the association posts. I could be anywhere. Not this overgrown farmers' town with its couple of cheesy gay bars and stinky bathhouse and lonely homos. In Vic Park the other night, a guy was sucking my cock, and suddenly I recognized him.

"Benny Jensen!" I'd said. "How's the arm?"

I was so glad he was alive. I held Benny's head in the dark, his soft hair and sweaty scalp. I'd walked out of the bar by myself one night in early spring and seen him stumbling down the street. By the time I'd caught up to him I'd realized he wasn't just drunk. He had a black eye and was cradling his forearm. I got him into a taxi and brought him to Emergency. Biting into his own fist to try to stave off the pain. I tried to stay with him but once he'd been through triage he thanked me and begged me to please leave.

"What happened?" I'd asked, on the way to the hospital.

"Fell off my skateboard."

I was kind of drunk myself, and not sure of things.

"The streets are still icy, Benny."

At the breakfast table, Ted pours mimosas. Mel asks who wants to join her for an easy six miles and we both do. It's a struggle for Ted and me to keep up, though.

When we return, Mel takes the first shower while Ted and I stretch on the deck. He's wearing just his gym shorts, and sweat pours off his muscled back when he bends over to work on his hamstrings. I want to climb on top and slide all over. I will never be satisfied with anything.

If I moved away, I could live in a real Boystown somewhere. It's not really my kind of scene before but I could adjust, and meet some bona fide faggots. I could move to back to Toronto. I could move to Montreal. "I'm thinking of leaving permanently this time," I say.

Ted looks at me in his overheated daze and says he could go with me, but I know it's just a tiny part of him talking. The part that wants to be with me.

SORRY ISN'T GOOD ENOUGH

I WALK ONTO THE PLANE for the briefing and here is Charlene after ten years. I haven't seen her since we were hired. They recruited her straight from her reserve, a poster child for diversity—beautiful and kind and a quick study. She never spoke in class, though. Our instructor, Dave, was always telling increasingly made-up anecdotes about his own experiences (One: On a flight to Lima, a passenger had been waiting for his call light to be answered. When Dave finally appeared, the passenger said, "I've been fingering you for ten minutes and you haven't come." Two: On a flight to Delhi, a passenger said, "In my country you people are servants" and Dave replied, "In *my* country you people are taxi drivers." I'll bet, Dave.). In front of all of us, Dave asked Charlene why she never contributed to the discussion. She looked at him evenly and said she couldn't compete with his stories.

Now she lives in a townhouse in Port Credit. She holds out

her iPhone to show me a picture of her husband and her sheltie. On her days off, she's a physiotherapist. She looks different, not just ten years older. The way she's shaped her eyebrows, her make-up and everything have taken away her Native look. She's another pretty stewardess now.

The purser, Gloria, walks on a few minutes later in a huff of luggage—purse, lunch cooler, laptop bag, suitcase, tote, parka. She's petite and heavily bejewelled, insultingly red fresh lipstick leaving a smudge on her bleached fangs. She's in her mid-forties.

"Excuse my tardiness," she says. "Traffic!"

She starts to put her stuff away in the closet that is reserved for passengers, throwing everything on top of the first aid kit, the bottles of water, and the newspapers that I'm supposed to distribute later. I don't think of that now, but I'll remember when my face is buried in the smell of cheaply dry-cleaned tweed jackets, and I have to move all her crap out of the way just to get some dufus an aspirin.

When we are in the air and I'm selling the food off the trolley, I see Mike for the first time since high school and he tells me about the cancer lab he's opened at U of T. He's married to Karen, whom I used to hang with. Everyone thought her and her sister and I were having threesomes, but we would just exercise and bake cakes and make each other friendship bracelets. We ran in the trails behind the school in the fall, the bolts of orange and red backlit by cold sun. The girls' blonde ponytails bounced in synch with their strides, small gold hoop earrings glinting. They were beautiful, no question, like Russian tennis stars. We'd always push hard through the flat poplar grove, our eyes and cheeks burning salt in the yellow glow. I never take in the sweet stink of mulch without remembering their soft footsteps, scattering leaves. We lived in a small northern paradise and there was no question we would move on, that we would wrench ourselves from where we began like transplanted shrubs, never minding the incompatibilities. Karen and Jessica were star athletes but I could keep up with them because I was a boy and puberty had hit suddenly, its shock of force filling me with unearned strength. My father walked me up and down the hall in the middle of the night —my quickly-sprouting legs as agonized as if they'd been on a stretching rack. When the time was right, when my peach fuzz and armpits began to ripen, he bought me a shaving kit, lovingly stocked and presented to me in front of the family at breakfast. I was ashamed and embarrassed, perhaps knowing what travails lay ahead.

After I finish picking up the garbage, I grab a beer for Mike and invite him to sit with me in the crew seats. His paw dwarfs the can. He fills me in—he and Karen have a baby and a toddler and they live in the Annex. He shows me a picture of everybody on the back deck. I can tell the lawn furniture is expensive even from the photograph. Jessica works way up north, further north then where we grew up, as far as you can go and still be near a good hospital because now she's a doctor. She sets up blood clinics and AIDS awareness programs for First Nations and clinics for prostitutes. She was brilliant in school but high-strung, never even joining us in a campfire toke. If she even dared to try a cooler at a party she'd go on about how drunk she was. The guys liked her, though there was never anyone serious. She flies south once a month for a long weekend because she loves spending time with Mike and Karen's kids.

She doesn't have any of her own.

No boyfriends, either.

"She's had three lesbian lovers," says Mike. The first one was much older, the second one lived in the bush with no electricity and it became too rustic, the third one lasted the longest but it didn't work out, either. In any case, she's still exploring, she doesn't know whether she's gay or bisexual or what, like a word will solve it, like nobody's ever heard of deconstructionism.

"She's lucky we're so open-minded," says Mike, and of course I nod, because I have always been agreeable. I used to see those ads for assertiveness training on the subway posters and would think about signing up but really, your personality is yours to keep and I've gotten used to mine. It's kept me employed, even if it doesn't make me a leader, but then we can't all be that, all going off to development camps and devising plans to save the world, nobody listening or following because they are all trying to get everyone else to comply with their own brilliant suggestions. *Send your daughter to our bullshit school, the world needs her.* Pictures of melting icecaps and starving babies, they must have been happy when the oil spilled, what scenic aerials! What a lot of pressure on those girls—their parents probably have all sorts of goals for them—athletic scholarships, through they're the last ones to need them, and after that medicine or law or business. It never changes. Then the Forty under 40 list. Something inside me curdles when I read about their life philosophies and biggest influences and that column where they list their charity work. They're probably all fucking around on their spouses and snorting coke at parties. *I am so blessed, I just want to give back, I just want to make a difference.*

Or maybe I'm just jealous. Jessica could be on one of those lists. Mike, too.

I glance over at him. He seems genuinely glad to see me. He's forgotten or revised the New Year's in Grade Twelve when we sat up after everyone else had gone to bed, so stoned, playing 45s—they were retro even then—the Kinks, the Clash, Concrete Blond singing *Everybody Knows*, none of us even knowing it was a cover. Bonding. It was a breakthrough, the gifted captain of the basketball team and the not-unpopular, nice, mild, gay guy. I'd tried out for basketball myself but never made the cut. I could manage pick-up with Karen and Jessica but that wasn't going to help me with the big guys. That feeling like you're not good enough, like you're missing out. I realize just now that it never really goes away.

Mike and I talked all night. We were both so unformed, despite his rock-hard smokin' bod. We were just wearing our jeans because all the boys had taken off their shirts to go have a fight in the snow after we'd worked up a sweat dancing. He was bragging, or showing off, telling me how he liked to put his finger up this chick's butt just as she was coming.

I said, you're distracting me. You should put on a shirt.

He took offense.

"Why'd you have to say that?" he said. "Why? We were having such a good time." And I said sorry. I was always apologizing in those days, so obsequious, like when people told me it was okay with them if I was gay so long as I kept the details to myself. Stupidly grateful.

I left the party and walked home through the slush. It's always grey on New Year's morning. The invitation to join Mike and his friends on their ice-fishing trip over the rest of the school holidays was implicitly revoked, but I went over the next day to try to patch things up anyway. We didn't even get down to it, even though Mike was the type of salt-of-the-earth guy who always wanted to get over every problem right away. We never saw much of each other after that.

On the plane, underneath us, the floor shifts. We are descending, so Mike goes back to his seat. Say hi to Karen, I say. And Jessica. And Mike says sure, nice running into you. You look the same.

We land in Edmonton, get in the van and watch a stark winter sunset on the long highway drive to the crappy hotel, in between the Canadian Superstore and the Costco. Last time they only had handicapped rooms left. My room was above the 'I' on the 'Inn' part of the sign. Everything was carefully laid out around the edges of the room—low table, low nightstand, low desk, low bed with railing assist on the wall—all bathed in green light from outside.

The carpet was so used it was shiny. I lay down on it and practised my abdominal breathing and worked on my non-attachment to the ebbs and flows of fortune.

Charlene and I and the first officer are watching the sky change from washed-out pink to purple to black, the tin-wire stars just hanging. I see a lot of neat sunsets. Gloria and the captain are telling jokes.

"What did the Indian say when he saw his first pizza?" asks Gloria, and the captain says something lame like where's the beer to go with it and Gloria says, "No, no—who puked on the bannock?!?" and they laugh and I feel uneasy.

Then the captain says that incestuous one about the girl and the crushed smokes and they laugh meanly and Charlene has turned to stone and I take a deep breath or forget to breathe, I don't remember.

"You might want to sign up for some sensitivity training," I say. "You might want to act more professional-like."

A pause. Gloria looks down and mumbles something, a defensive rebuttal or embarrassed apology. It doesn't matter, she knows she shouldn't have.

And the captain says, "You're right. I'm sorry." And I realize he is. He's just an old redneck on the verge or retirement. He probably learned to fly in the military and then worked bush planes when he got out, fixing the engines himself. Maybe he got to fish sometimes. Were there any women or did he just use magazines? How foreign and bizarre we must seem to him, sipping our skinny lattes and running off for sushi in the Vancouver airport, the male flight attendants gushing about getting engaged to each other and the women flaunting their masters' degrees, consulting on the side, the flying gig just an excuse to get away from their husbands.

Or maybe I'm just making assumptions.

And I thought there is no point telling them Charlene is

native herself. That shouldn't matter and anyway it's her call, it would be *disempowering*, right? No wonder we're all getting stupider, nobody wants any decisions made on their behalf, as if people would willingly learn to differentiate equations, or learn to conjugate terrible French verbs. Chemical titrations just for kicks. But somebody's got to learn.

I thought that would be the end of my admonition but more words spilled out. Why can't every day be like this?

"Sorry isn't good enough, you'd have gone right ahead if I wasn't here. What year is this, that you've never heard of respect?" I say they're lucky I don't give enough of a shit about this airline to bother reporting them.

What a trip. What a strange and pious and sickening way to get a rush.

I hurry up to my hotel room, avoiding the others and this time it's a regular one with no green glow and my legs are shaking and I feel great, like I've just parachuted. I take off all my clothes except my boxers and look in the mirror. I've been overeating lately, bored at work so I gorge on all those fake potato chips and salted cashews and leftover pizzas from the food cart. My belly's gone soft but it's still flat. I pop a few Advil and drink a few splits of wine I swiped off the plane and I turn up the heat and do push-ups and sit-ups and burpees until I puke, then I do some more. I'm out for blood.

When I reach failure, I watch a few *Family Guy* episodes and then crash. I wake up thirsty a few times, but I'm too lazy to get up for water.

I remember the last dream I have before morning. I dream my friend's baby has hit his head on a stone floor.

"Don't let him go to sleep," I say. "Don't let him go to sleep!" But then he's unconscious. Then he's not breathing. I give mouth-to-mouth and I can feel that he's gone cold. I hold his delicate body in my arms. I cup his tiny head and scream for directions to the hospital but there are hedge mazes and wide, busy traffic lanes and long palace corridors and nobody can help me, nobody knows where to go. I run and run, searching, and my friend trails behind, unfazed and calm.

"Where is the fucking hospital?" I'm crying so hard. I don't want to face the truth.

My friend is right behind me, watching over. She doesn't seem upset, even though in real life I know she loves her son like the mother of a cub. She has native blood herself, long raven hair. She can sit by the fire for hours and it calms me.

In my dream I am so mournful. I don't want to lose this life.

"Don't worry," my friend says, "don't worry." She is patient, almost smiling. And then right before I wake up, she tells me there will always be another.

TELL THEM WHAT YOU NEED

SEAN WANTED TO MEET UP for friendly whiskeys at the strip club and over the table he put his hands on top of mine and looked right at me with his gentle grey eyes and I'd had no idea, none at all. One of the dancers came by to chat. He wore a construction hat over his acned, buck-toothed mug. Ill-fitting Levi's and work boots. He was sexy, though. Sexual.

He leaned onto our table, faux-casual. Sean removed his hands from mine and spoke to him.

"When are you up?"

"Not the next guy but right after."

"You do lap dances?"

"Yeah...you want one?"

"Another night, man. You in this full-time?"

"No, I'm in college."

"Taking what?"

"Recreation and leisure."

"This some type of practical component?"

He didn't get it, but I laughed.

I had to fly early the next morning, so I called it a night. Sean walked me home and said he wished he could go with me. I didn't know whether he meant upstairs to my apartment, or far away.

That was months ago. Since then there have been a few hijinks on my couch—pants off, cocks in mouths. Mostly just fooling around. Sean is so strong and tall and outgoing, but he likes to be still while I touch him. My hands run all over his body while he holds me around the waist, eyes closed. Once, in my kitchen, he lets me fuck him, our pants lying in piles around our ankles.

"I needed that," he says, right after. I want him to stay over but by the time I think to ask his jeans are up and fastened and his belt is buckled.

I have a layover in Montreal. I don't get to the hotel until midnight, but as soon as I'm in my room I doff my scratchy, coffee-stained uniform. Then I throw on some cargo pants and a t-shirt and head over to Ste-Catherine to check out the strippers. I text him, just to touch base.

French peelers are the best, man! Get a lap dance.

But I don't. I don't know what happens or how it works. I'd like to ask him how to go about it.

Whatever you want—you're paying. Tell them what you need.

Now he is going shopping at the new high-end grocery store near my place.

Come join, he texts. I don't really need anything but I make a quick list and head over. We check out the produce. He picks out a rambutan and a couple of jackfruits. At the lunch counter we get quinoa salad and lychee soup, and sit down to dine.

We are subdued while we eat. "I feel like I can be myself around you," he says.

Then he says, "Oh my God—I would love to fuck that guy behind the cheese counter." He goes right up to the guy and gets his number. The cheese guy looks startled at first, but he's grinning by the time Sean comes back to sit down.

Every day I wonder if my feelings for him will go away and every day the answer is no. Whenever I get home I strip down to my underwear and walk around the apartment and look closely at my own reflection.

I love you! I say to the guy in the mirror. (I didn't think of this myself. It was something I overheard from one of the girls at work.)

Then there's my job. Nobody gives a shit about anything at this airline. The duty manager this morning gives me a once over.

"Your eyes are very red."

"Oh, I know," I say. "They're so dry!"

She doesn't want to deal with it. Still, I am cautious when I walk onto the plane. But I know Greg, the purser, and Brent, and they are both cool.

"Brent," says Greg, "I'm gonna leave Henry out of sight in the galley. You'll work the aisle."

Brent has a thick brushcut and a small wrestler's body. He tries to act all butch but I've seen him with the passengers.

Oh my God, I love your shoes!

Is the tea still hot? Fluttering his lovely eyelashes.

I wouldn't say he's a passive queer, though. Last time, I opened the door to come out of the lavatory and he guided me right back in.

I wanna suck your cock, man.

So he did.

I go to the back and start arranging the coffee pots and juice boxes. I turn on the ovens. This airline still gives out omelettes on some flights, in little square dishes. Then they throw the dishes out because everything is made of plastic. It's okay though—*they plant trees.*

The passengers struggle with their bags. There is nowhere to put anything and yeah yeah it's the last time they'll fly charter. I thought Sean was falling in love with me but he didn't, and now I'm thrown off.

There is only one person in the last row—Maggie. She boarded ahead of the rest because she has a brain injury. I ask her if she wants anything.

She says, "I want you to sit beside me for a bit." So I do. It's not something I would request myself but I appreciate her honesty. You won't catch me asking some guy for comfort.

I need affection.

It would sound funny.

Hold me.

I used to laugh at stuff like that because most guys fuck and leave. Or tell you to go. They don't tell you how comfortable they feel around you.

I need to get some sleep, bro! That was nice, though.

Not like Maggie here—she is going on about her relatives in Corner Brook and now she leans in and rests her shoulder against mine. She looks up at me and gives me a buddy grin.

"I know what's going on," she says. She is cross-eyed and I keep switching, unsure. "Don't worry. I like you."

I like you.

I leave Maggie so that I can arm the slides on the doors and finish my prep work. At the front, in front of everyone, Brent is fastening a seatbelt that is attached to nothing. He is pointing out exits, putting on a lifevest. It is so thrilling and nobody sees.

I am reeling slightly so I pop a clorazepam. I can't wait to get to the hotel so I can have a few more. I look over my shoulder and Maggie gives me a wink.

We take off. In my jumpseat I stretch out my legs. Lately I have been so cramped. I have been getting the most relentless charley horses, out of the blue. I don't know how to stop them—I stretch more, I try magnesium and drink chicken broth and Gatorade and use ice and heat but still my calf seizes up and I can only observe the misshapen form that is my leg. Such bizarre, painful contortions, like witches' limbs or horror-flick tree branches. I gasp at the big indentations between the frozen muscles while I wait for the agony to subside.

I smell cheap egg. This morning I got up early and rolled a skunky spliff and smoked it on the balcony and thought *I will have a wake and bake and book off sick*, but I forgot to book off. Then at Keele the subway came aboveground and the sun was shining and I was starting to really buzz and Sean was sitting beside me with his hand resting on my thigh and we were going on a trip and I had to look out the window because I was so grateful and bedazzled and when I turned back he was not there.

We are climbing higher, through the barely-there clouds. Solid columns of sun spear through the windows. Tomorrow night when I get home I will roll a king-sized joint. I will crank up some tunes and do my *I love you* thing.

Brent stares at me from his jumpseat. I watch him while I grab my crotch. I give a little tug.

Yeah.

Then suddenly I am very tired. The seatbelt sign turns off but nobody gets up. I look over at Brent and his lust for me is extinguished. He is zoned out and there is a high-pitched screech coming from a door seal somewhere and this is an emergency and the urge to grab Sean tight immobilizes me, heavy as an anvil, but then I remember the procedures, the oxygen. The masks have not dropped so I punch my pen through the stupid release hole in the panel. My mask falls out and I put it on and take a nice breath and this should have happened sooner, because now I could tell him something. He told me he couldn't stop thinking about me. He only said it once and I couldn't grasp it and I said nothing. I help Brent with his mask and his eyelids flutter again and I think *Wake up, Sleeping Beauty*! We grab the portable tanks and go from row to row, shoving pens in the holes—oh why oh why do things never work?—and putting the masks on people's faces and the people are so beautiful and dazed. One by one they turn from blue to pink and each time is a promise.

I get to Maggie. I should have helped her first but I started at the wrong end. She springs to life faster than the others, though. Even with her yellow duck mask on I can tell she is smiling at all the fun.

From the flight deck comes a pledge, hesitant and muffled. Greg signals for us to station up. I head to my jumpseat but Maggie pats the space beside her and gestures for me to sit. I think of Sean but it is Maggie who is going to save me, and where is Sean? Is he getting a lap dance? Is he fucking the cheese guy? Maybe he is telling somebody that he can be himself around him. Maybe he is holding someone's hands, right on top of the table.

Maggie keeps me in her crooked gaze. The plane is thumping like a speedboat crossing jagged waves and we are going down faster than we went up. The door and the people are shrieking. I think about Sean all the time, does he even know that? All the time.

I don't feel stoned at all. I look into the eye that winked and I reach out.

Now, I think. *Now I am asking.*

127

PEOPLE SHOULD DO WHAT THEY WANT

Russ used to come over to my hotel room, cold six-pack in hand, whenever my job sent me to Vancouver. We'd be finishing up the last two cans, talking out of our asses—really good free-flowing conversation, the kind you don't realize you've been craving until you're getting it. Then he'd lean over and start in on me. The sex was primal and animalistic and there was no question of who was going to get fucked. After, he wouldn't let go. Sometimes he made me face him all night; he said he wanted to breathe me in. I'll never let anyone say that to me again.

He only did what he wanted, all the time. Sullen, but when he smiled you knew he meant it. Cigarette smoke seeped from him, he drank steadily, he'd try any drug, but he never lost control. When he thought to eat it was chips or candy, sometimes a steak. The body of a Greek god, even though he'd probably never been inside a weight room. He didn't need that prissy stuff. Pierced tongue, tattoo, shaved head, fuck you. Physicality incarnate, lying in my bed.

In the morning, I'd wake up with my head on his perfect chest. He'd light a cigarette at the window while I made coffee in the little pot they always put in the rooms. I guess I started smoking as a way to emulate him. I'd always been a good, earnest kid, stayed away from the bad boys even though I was drawn to them. They hung out at the south end of our school, smoking and snarling in their stuffed jeans and black leather jackets, and I was afraid. Officially, they were losers but I always knew they were better than me, more alive. They didn't follow the rules. I only had to walk past them occasionally and sometimes one of them would say, "wuss," or "fag," but I just absorbed it, kept walking.

When the coffee was brewed Russ would pull out a flask of brandy and pour generous amounts. "This'll give it a kick," he'd say and we'd clink our mugs. It was his favourite way to start the day, but sometimes I had to refuse. I couldn't have alcohol before work, and he'd sneer, like the time he saw a mutual fund brochure sticking out of my bag. He's an installation artist, he has an eye and he picks heavy stuff up and rearranges it. He lives hand to mouth and if he's short at the end of the month he deals with it— builds a deck, turns over some drugs, whatever it takes.

I got really into him very quickly. It was completely out of my control. He didn't seem like the kind of guy who would have sex because he was wasted or bored or feeling obligated. When he'd come for me it was like he'd kill for it, and I let that get to my head.

Russ got into some project out on the island for a month, something vague and industrial. He said we'd catch up, for sure, next time we were both back in Vancouver. After the month, I left a few messages to say when I was coming to town but he never returned them. I am not a stalker, but I missed him. But I am not a stalker.

So I left it at that and tried to suck it up. I started to smoke a bit more, like him. Pour brandy in my coffee every day. Three sheets to the wind—it maybe wasn't as becoming on me.

My doctor eyed me up and down: thinner in the wrong parts, bloodshot eyes, rough skin. It's funny, I'd never felt like a nice piece of meat until I met Russ, and that was when I started to let it all go. My doctor wanted to know things, such as what were my feelings like these days. I tried to explain, but I just shuddered, couldn't talk. "Do you think this is a chemical or situational thing?" asked my doctor.

Both, I wanted to say. My chemistry's been altered because of the situation. Every atom is fixated on one guy. If he goes west they all turn that way, reaching. His pull is way too strong.

If you perk up your ears, news just comes to you. I hear that Russ has moved to Toronto, and that he has a favourite hangout near the house I share in Kensington Market. I down a few beers at home, my roommates eyeing me nervously, then head out. It's cold so I put my hands in my armpits. Russ is not the kind of guy you want to meet up with if you have cold hands.

OK, so it was more than a few beers. I stumble into the bar. Russ is sitting alone, content and drunk, too. He's glad to see me because I'm that kind of a guy. Easygoing or self-effacing, I'm never sure. They like to cut me off at the waist when they're done with the sex, though. Pretend I don't have a dick. I shouldn't let them do that.

I was smart to keep my hands warm. When he gives me a friendly hug I can't help touching his thick neck. He buys me a drink. There is no mention of any unfinished business because he does what he wants without apology. That was part of the attraction. To ask about unreturned calls would betray the whole relationship; people should do what they want.

We shoot the shit like old times, disprove karma, solve the energy crisis. The beer is going down fast but we have to step outside for a smoke and we just keep walking, why not. It's still early and we are two young men hitting the town.

We pass an old house on Baldwin and Russ looks up at the second floor balcony and smiles and shakes his head, reminiscing. He says he paid a visit to a guy's apartment here, when he was a teenager. He is remembering some passionate encounter, and I turn quiet. When I was his age, I went to swim practice and track, piano and math club. I won the citizenship award—what a joke. I bought into all of it, took it into the pool, tried to sublimate everything into a faster 1500, into arpeggios and exponential equations. That was a huge mistake and I'm still learning now, still catching up. I never went over to someone's house after class, not like that. Since I've met him it cuts the shit out of me, all that wasted time. Russ was like the baddest, sexiest kid in school, telling me to come over.

We stop at a dive in Chinatown for a few cans of Bud, ask the waiter to bring the next round unopened. We pay and stuff the cans into our coats on the way out. Outside, we sip and walk. We are thoroughly blitzed, and I am in full wandering mode, jumping over fences haphazardly, through building sites, dark alleys. Russ follows. We climb up the stairs to the deserted public square behind City Hall. It's getting colder and the concrete reflects sodium orange into the black night.

I try to kiss him, like he used to do to me, but he moves his head out of the way.

"Don't do that," he says quietly, bored, no trace of a threat. The words leave his mouth in a stream of frost. Whatever it was is over anyway, so I can't help asking now. I don't want to break any unspoken terms but I need words, I say. An explanation. Was it something I did?

I understand the futility of the question. Russ is completely unaffected. "I never thought we were anything more than friends," he says, but I've tried that, I've fooled around with friends and it was never anything more than friendly. I never wanted to breathe them in all night. Is that all he thought of me? This is some type of devastation; I can't apologize for being upset.

In front of him, though, I hold it all in. I drop him off at home and by the time I get to my place I am a mess, yelling and crying, lighting the filter end of the cigarette. Grief, or something else, I haven't been sure of anything in a long time. My roommates are nonplussed, especially when I smash a hole through the bedroom wall, the first bloody knuckles of my life. I keep going outside to puke but the air has snapped, it's arctic, they keep hauling me back in. My roommates are quiet types, like me. In no way do they find this amusing. I suppose they are tired of returning from work to see that I've stayed home to enjoy a bottle of Pinot Noir and some sleeping pills and to clutch my head in my hands all day. But somebody should see. Tomorrow they can kick me out, or I can offer to leave. I'll get my own place, keep my expenses down. I don't need much anyway, just a good fuck now and then and you don't pay for that with money.

Tonight I don't care about that, though. Something red and enraged has been plucked and squeezed raw. It was pus-filled, it has spread everywhere and I want everyone to know that I am not fucking happy. When I finally stop ranting, it is deemed safe to leave me alone in my bedroom with a towel and a bucket.

I leave the light on, lick the salty blood from the back of my hand while I stare at the hole in the wall. I did that. Shame and pride. You're not supposed to put holes in things, despite the satisfaction therein derived. I wanted guidelines.

And I never should have just taken everything in, because now it's all going to have to come back out.

ANYBODY WHO SHOWS UP IS WELCOME

MR. SHARPE SEES ME SMOKING in the parking lot at the mall. He comes right over, takes the cigarette out of my hand and stomps it on the ground, laughs.

"Moss," he says, "it's so good to see you. I heard you were back in town." So he knows. I guess word travels fast. The gay fuck-up has cracked and has moved back to live with his parents. Stress leave is the official explanation.

"Hello," I say. "It's good to see *you*, Sir!" He was the only teacher we addressed that way. He insisted on it.

"Moss," he says again. He always loved saying my name. I stared at his crotch all through Grade Nine. What teachers must think of us, what they must know and see. It's fifteen years later.

"I heard things got a little rough for you down south."

"That's right. But I'm working things out!" I try to be bright

133

when I say this. To lack enthusiasm around him was worse than swearing. You'd be in less trouble if you came to class drunk. I only ever dozed off once. He stopped explaining whatever theorem we were working on and just stared at me. The class was silent. I felt my eyes sting and my face prickling with heat and turning cherry red.

"I know you will. We need an assistant coach for girls' cross-country. You don't have to do much, just run with them. Might get you back into shape, mister." He eyes the cigarette on the ground. I haven't run in years, unless the beer store was about to close. I haven't gotten fat, but maybe that's the smoking. "It's only five runs a week, Moss. After school. You got the time?" The unspoken impli-cation. Of course I do. No commitments at all except therapy twice a week. The social worker from Employee Assistance is quiet and attentive. I usually shed a few tears, boo hoo. Then she'll say we're making good progress. After a session, I feel better for about an hour.

I don't want to help but I could never say no to Mr. Sharpe. He was the one who got me involved in running in the first place, made sure I was at all the practices even though he coached the girls.

"A boy needs an outlet," he always said. It's true that he took a special interest in me. I worked so hard for him in class. Always did my homework, every problem worked out properly and copied neat. If I couldn't solve even one, I'd be at school an hour early, ready to go over it with him. I used to help on his farm on the weekends with the the sled dogs and horses. He said he needed fit people to run the animals, and at the time I was. I ached to be him, or to be with him, or something. He must be sixty now, but he still has a six-pack. When he smiles in his zany way you can see chipped front teeth from when one of the horses trampled him. Crazy, intelligent bug eyes and an Olympian metabolism. I guess he won't retire until they force him out.

I go down to the lake that night and sit on my favourite rock and smoke my last cigarette. I'll miss the ludicrous high that first drag can give you. When everything spins.

Part of me wants to be miserable and loyal to you, and part of me wants to move on.

The first day of school is a Tuesday afternoon. I meet the girls and Mr. Sharpe on the track. We'll all run together today—the midgets, juniors and seniors—an easy three miles. The girls are mostly tall and thin and they've heard of me, their oldest siblings know my youngest brother or someone told them I was a homo or a varsity athlete or that I'd been dumped and gone off the rocks or some combination thereof. I've been living in different cities since I finished high school.

It's hot and we jog lightly along the base of the escarpment. Mr. Sharpe makes declarations on technique, team loyalty, toughness. The plan is for me to take the seniors for longer runs on trail days, while he sticks with the young ones. I can already see who the scorers will be: they wear the same ponytails and chat together up front, barely breaking a sweat. They've been competing in track all summer. A few of them are a bit serious but most of them just want to be in shape. They seem beautiful and confident and friendly and I wonder if that's how they feel.

I am heaving mid-pack, trying to joke with the fast runners and encourage the slow. Mr. Sharpe is at the rear, barking out instructions, plans for the season. The students still call him Sir. For a few seconds I drift and I think about you and how you said sorry, you had fallen for someone else and you said it like a chore, because you just wanted to get back to him, didn't you? But then I catch myself and focus on the girls, the running, the running. I am barely a coach, more like a tag-along, but they don't seem to mind. After all, it's not some higher institute of sport, it's a high school cross-country squad in East Shore. Anybody who shows up is welcome, even me.

135

* * *

I settle into a routine. Chores in the morning for my mom and dad, then after lunch a nap unless I have to chat with the shrink. A bit of stretching before practice, then run. The runs start to get harder, and this induces a pain that is nostalgic. We've broken up into packs now, so it's just me and the seniors, eight tall thin young women and a taller, thinner man.

When I first came home I couldn't eat much. They made me sit down to dinner, though. Crying into my plate, right in front of them. The tears falling on the white china, lovely rivulets streaming into the asparagus. What do parents endure? Do they have any idea beforehand? I'll never have kids; I wouldn't be able to stand it.

I have never had to deal with what you are going through, said my mother.

The hills heave upwards, shudder and flatten as we approach, darkened trails like veins. The autumn colours are as basic as a cartoon and the sun scorches but it is cool underneath the trees. Every step is seared in. I keep us together, a sheep herder. I run stronger and faster and think of you and force my thoughts back to the girls. I haven't had a cigarette in almost three weeks and already I'm fitter than I've been in years and the girls and I banter and laugh. When you told me you didn't love me I tried to be strong but you had become everything. How did that happen? I tried to make some friends then but nobody else seemed good enough compared to you. You called occasionally after you moved out and that was well-intended, but you shouldn't have because it sent me back to zero every time. Those times you came over to check up on me, I really was just about to clean the place up and get the mail. I know I had used up my sick days and I know it didn't look good but the intention to get my shit together was there.

We stretch after practice in the grass by the football field, amidst water bottles and sports bags, listening to Mr. Sharpe's rants and raves. I am one of them now, a young runner. Not quite a friend and not quite a coach. Tomorrow we'll do six eight-hundreds on the track and that will hurt. I've started doing the speedwork sessions with them even though I was supposed to just keep track of splits. I've gotten competitive with them and we're all enjoying it and you will never be mine again, you never were. I will dig as hard as I did fifteen years ago and you will not be there, you could not care less. You gave me something that made everything else seem like nothing and then you took it away.

The girls turn into people for me. Sally is the cheekiest, freckles and love; she pinches my shoulder and tells me to get moving on a long uphill. Gina's boyfriend wants to have sex and she's not sure. I'm surprised but don't admit it. I thought they were all doing that stuff already. Linda talks to me after practice because her mom has just come out of the closet. I hadn't heard about that. She has questions, or just wants to chat, so I let her. I can't do much else for her. I know dick-all about relationships so I just let her feel her way around things.

"Why did she lie to us for so long?" she asks.

"Maybe she was afraid," I tell her. "Maybe she was afraid you wouldn't love her anymore."

They experiment with their confidences. Some of them smoke pot. Daring to talk about it in front of Mr. Moss is part of the fun, but I am not the teacher so I don't say anything either way. I don't smoke it myself anymore because it just makes me sleepy. I could have used more of it as a teenager though, for sure. No one likes to admit it, but there are reasons why the cool kids are cool.

Our first race is this Saturday. Everyone is tired and a bit overtrained and I convince Mr. Sharpe to let us replace a tempo run with a yoga class.

The team is keen to try. This is different than the classes I went to in Toronto, when I was alone again. Those ones had tea tree candles, recycled wide-plank oak floors, subdued lighting. Buddhist monks chanted over the expensive sound system. The other students wore hundred dollar tights and were as hard as diamonds, never smiling or saying hello. I know yoga isn't for meeting people, but I could have used some eye contact, some innocuous greetings.

Hello. Nice to see you again. How are you doing?

We are in the school gym. The girls are wearing boxer shorts over bathing suits and lying on smelly wrestling mats. Braces flash and without Mr. Sharpe's presence there are giggles and whispering. I tell them to settle down. For a second one will become a woman out of the corner of my eye but when I focus in she's a girl again. They must drive their parents crazy.

I lead everyone through some simple sun salutations, and then we go through the warrior sequence and do a few standing balances and some seated forward bends. I tell them to focus on their breath and not each other and they seem to get something out of it but a few times there are more giggles.

Mr. Sharpe asks me how it went, after.

"Pretty well, sir. I think some of them might have been a bit self-conscious."

"That's okay, Moss," he says, nodding sagely. "Young people are more concerned with what's going on around them. It's only as we get older that we start to look within."

I wonder why anyone would ever want to do that.

I'll admit I was having difficulties. I know that's why you called my parents.

He's Having a Nervous Breakdown, you told them, and I wonder if at first it sounded comical. When we were kids we used to tell each other to not spazz out. *Don't have a nervous breakdown, dude.*

My dad drove all night to come get me. In the morning we met in the office with the union rep and my manager and worked out a plan to get back on my feet. I couldn't believe it was happening.

On the long drive home I looked over once. Deep bags under my father's eyes. He was in the army until his late thirties. Then he went back to school and became a teacher. He faced forward, concentrating on the road ahead.

Saturday race day. In this district, senior girls race five kilometres. I lead them over the whole course for warm-up, a long ragged loop around the old dump and then a quick up and down of the small ski hill. We stretch together and then I have them do a few windsprints before the start. They race well, and there are a few small dramas. Sally falls on the downhill and scrapes her elbows and knees raw, but she gets right back up and still comes in a quarter way through the pack.

Gina loses a shoe in the shallow creek and drops out.

After, Mr. Sharpe debriefs the team. He says it's a very tough course.

We soldier on in training. The trail runs get longer but on the track we do shorter intervals with more rest. We do an easy jog for twenty minutes, then eight four-hundreds all-out with two minutes rest after each. I think of you on the second last one, and realize it's been some time now.

Mr. Sharpe tells me I'm looking good.

"You'd better not head back south before district championships," he tells me. "The girls like you having you around." But he knows I won't be leaving that soon. Cross-country season is short up here. Winter comes early. There's only two weeks left in the season and I don't want it to end.

You are not mine and I know you never will be but there are

other ways to try and get something good out of life. You are not the be-all and end-all of my existence.

One more four-hundred. Sally usually beats everyone on short intervals. But I cross the line with her on this one, my best time of the whole workout.

She slaps my ass and tells me good work. I hesitate because I'm older, male, and because I'm in a position of semi-authority, but then I slap her ass back. Good work yourself, girl. She laughs. I'll have to remember to trust the whole context. To know that it's okay to show a little affection.

It's the district finals, and I am not a runner today. I am most definitely the assistant coach. I go over the race plans that Mr. Sharpe has carefully constructed. I yell out splits and encouragement. They really go for it. I love the look on the face of a good racer, such relaxation and concentration in the midst of overwhelming pain.

The seniors come in third, two places better than last year.

I really enjoyed my time with all of you, I tell them. I can feel something cracking in my throat but it's just a warm feeling. Something I'd forgotten about.

We'll miss you, Mr. Moss, they say but I can tell they're already thinking about volleyball tryouts and that's good.

Mr. Sharpe invites me over to do some chores around the farm before I go back to Toronto. The dogs are getting restless to pull the sled but it won't snow for a few more weeks. They've been running the trails around the property in the meantime, though, to get in shape.

They each have a little area and a doghouse to themselves in the trees behind the barn. We take them off their leashes to gather them for a pack run, but their eagerness and the presence of a visitor gets them strangely overexcited. Swiftly, without warning, they go over an edge, turn into a sickening mass of foaming black and white fur, enraged barking and agonized howls. They're ringing each other by the scruffs with their jaws. Droplets of blood fly through the air. It happens all at once.

Mr. Sharpe walks into the centre of the frenzy and expertly picks up the two worst offenders by their collars. He kicks at them until they ease up and then raises his arms while they thrash, commanding them in short and sharp words to calm the fuck down. Their teeth glisten bloody and shiny. I watch, unsure of what to do, while Mr. Sharpe stands in the centre of the writhing pile, arms outstretched, holding a dog by the scruff at each end. I will never be that kind of a man, I think.

"Moss!" he roars. His voice is as deep as God's. "Chain them up! Just rip them apart and get them leashed."

I try to order them to heel, to lie down but my voice compared to Mr. Sharpe's sounds like a girl's. So I pick away at the pack, one dog at a time. They can't bite you if you grab them by the scruff of the neck. It takes a couple of minutes but we manage to get them all released.

"Well," says Mr. Sharpe when it's all over. He's barely even breathing hard. His forehead is shiny and there are blood stains all over his jacket but he looks invigorated. "We may as well have lunch."

We go into the house and wash up and Mr. Sharpe makes chicken sandwiches while I put on the coffee.

We sit down to eat, laugh about the dogs. We chuckle the way men do when a violence is over. A tinge of relief, but no admission of weakness.

"You feeling better yet, Moss?" says Mr. Sharpe. He's not asking about the dogs. We've never been into the heavy stuff–even the jokes we tell each other are clean.

"I'm feeling pretty good, Sir."

"Glad to hear it. You're a grown man, now. You know that, eh?"

"Yes, Sir." If he's insinuating that I haven't been acting like one, I'm not offended. But I think it was more of an acknowledgement.

When I leave he walks me to the car and we shake hands. I start up while Mr. Sharpe stands over me at the driver's seat window, hands at his sides.

"I wouldn't want to see a man waste his life being sad, Moss. Good luck down there in the city."

I say yessir and thank him, and drive away.

Acknowledgements

THANK YOU TO MY WONDERFUL friend Angie Abdou, a founding member of my two-person writing group. Her longstanding habit of treating me as nothing less than a fellow author has done more for my writing than any workshop could.

My mother advised me to write as if she would never read it, and my father has shown by example that finding one's voice is cause for happiness in itself.

Dan Vos has shown me more love and kindness than I ever knew about.

Jayna Tyne's joy in my undertakings has reminded me to celebrate them. Tracy Sinclair has been a thoughtful first reader for some of the chapters. I have been supported by a gaggle of friends who make a good job of appearing to enjoy my stories and who welcome me back after my retreats into solitude and because I don't want to leave anyone out I am going to take the easy way and thank them all en masse.

Aunt Norma and Uncle Jim Kozma helped me to finish this book. Marina Endicott referred me to the world's best editor.

The publishers at Véhicule Press, Simon Dardick and Nancy Marrelli, gave me their trust. Several editors in the past encouraged me by publishing stories, especially Jeremy Hanson-Finger at *Dragnet Magazine*. Jess Taylor, Farzana Doctor and Dan Perry are three reasons why Toronto is a fertile, come-as-you-are place where writing thrives. Annabel Lyon mentored several chapters as part of UBC's Booming Ground program.

I saved Dimitri Nasrallah until the end of this list only so that he will stand out. I enjoyed our collaborative process. It is a unique privilege to work with someone of such scintillating intelligence and precise vision, and I am grateful for it.

ESPLANADE
Books

THE FICTION SERIES AT VÉHICULE PRESS

A House by the Sea : A novel by Sikeena Karmali

A Short Journey by Car : Stories by Liam Durcan

Seventeen Tomatoes : Tales from Kashmir : Stories by Jaspreet Singh

Garbage Head : A novel by Christopher Willard

The Rent Collector : A novel by B. Glen Rotchin

Dead Man's Float : A novel by Nicholas Maes

Optique : Stories by Clayton Bailey

Out of Cleveland : Stories by Lolette Kuby

Pardon Our Monsters : Stories by Andrew Hood

Chef : A novel by Jaspreet Singh

Orfeo : A novel by Hans-Jürgen Greif
[Translated by Fred A. Reed]

Anna's Shadow : A novel by David Manicom

Sundre : A novel by Christopher Willard

Animals : A novel by Don LePan

Writing Personals : A novel by Lolette Kuby

Niko : A novel by Dimitri Nasrallah

Stopping for Strangers : Stories by Daniel Griffin

The Love Monster : A novel by Missy Marston

A Message for the Emperor : A novel by Mark Frutkin

New Tab : A novel by Guillaume Morissette

Swing in the House and Other Stories : Anita Anand

Breathing Lessons : A novel by Andy Sinclair

Véhicule Press